SWEET MAGNOLIA

CHARLESTON HARBOR NOVELS

DEBBIE WHITE

ISBN - 9781983480928 KDP PAPERBACK

ISBN - 978-1-7363803-4-5 INGRAM SPARK PAPERBACK

SWEET MAGNOLIA

Editing provided by Daniela Prima of Prima Editing & Proofreading Services &

Leo Bricker of The Grammatical Eye®

Cover Design by Larry White

Debbie White Books

Summerville, South Carolina

CHAPTER 1

Thoroughly exhausted, but happy to be sitting in first class sipping cocktails, Annie rested her head back on the cushiony pillow casually turning her head toward Jack.

"I'm sitting here worried about, of all things, those darn porta potties," she said, knitting her brows together.

Jack patted her leg. "Don't worry about anything. We're on our honeymoon now."

Annie let out a sigh. "I know it's only a couple of days, but it will be heaven sitting on the veranda overlooking vineyards and sipping on chardonnay."

"On our next anniversary, we're going to Europe and will have a proper honeymoon," Jack said, leafing through the magazine he pulled from the seat pocket in front of him.

"This is a proper honeymoon, Jack." She nuzzled his arm and pulled him down, whispering in his ear.

Jack's eyes widened. "I like the way you think," he said, kissing her on the lips.

Their flight lasted about six hours and while they were tired, they were just as eager for all things cool, like chardonnay on the veranda, and all things warm and bubbly like a hot tub. They gathered their bags from the baggage claim area, picked up their rental car, and off they went in search of the quaint villa Jack had reserved.

It was dusk by the time they landed and making their way through San Francisco proved to be a bit challenging. Suffice to say, neither of them had seen traffic quite this bad before. Thank goodness for Google; Annie was able to guide Jack through the snarled roadway of cars, and soon the orange architectural icon known as the Golden Gate Bridge came into view.

"Oh, my. This is absolutely gorgeous," Annie said as she peered out the side window, looking up, down, and all around. "Look at the height of this bridge."

"It's so high up that it's shrouded in fog and looks like it goes on forever," Jack said, trying to keep his eyes on the lane ahead of him.

Leaning forward and looking out the windshield with her mouth agape, Annie said, "I know, right? It's like it dissolves into darkness. Wow, truly magnificent."

"This is one long bridge," Jack said as they crept along, in what they figured out to be the tail end of commuter traffic.

"I guess most of these people work in San Francisco and live in towns on the other side of the bridge," Annie said.

After they'd traveled the length of the bridge, they soon entered a tunnel. When they came out the other end, she noticed houseboats tied up. "Wow, look at that. There are lights on, so people are obviously living in them," Annie said, nodding toward the anchored boats. Her eyes followed the sign until they passed it. "Sausalito," she said out loud.

"I think I read somewhere that due to the outrageous rents here, many do live on houseboats," Jack said.

After they'd driven about ninety minutes, they began to look for signs that would lead them to the villa.

"Let's see. Not this exit but the next one," Annie said. "After this light, it looks like we make a left, drive about three miles, and then make a right."

Jack pulled up to a light-colored stucco building. A motion light came on when he parked in the driveway and lit up the place, almost blinding them.

"They are really into security here," he said.

"Oh, Jack, it's beautiful. It really does look like a villa in Italy somewhere."

"I picked it because of its location—we're close to many great wineries, the view, according to the website, is fabulous, and well, you know about the hot tub," he said, pulling her in and sneaking a kiss.

Jack took her hand in his, and they walked to the front door. "The key is supposed to be under the mat." He crouched over and pulled up the corner. He rolled his head to the right and smiled up at her as he presented the shiny metal key. "Ta-da," he said, waving it.

He put the key in the door and gave it a quick turn, pushing the door out of the way. Annie started to step forward, but he caught her around the waist. "Nope. Not yet," he said, picking her up in his arms. He stepped across the threshold and took a few steps before putting her down on the king-size bed. "I've been waiting to do that." He kissed her on the mouth.

Annie bounced on the bed and laughed. Patting the bed beside her with a look of sheer desire, she said, "Come here, my darling."

Jack stumbled and then collapsed next to her, pulling her on top. She placed her hands on his chest and gazed into his warm eyes. "Mrs. Powell. I'll never get tired of saying it." She lowered her mouth to his and kissed him deeply, dipping her tongue between the seams of his mouth.

"*Ahem.*"

Jack and Annie bolted straight up from their loving embrace. Annie smoothed down her clothes and hair, as Jack scooted off the bed and crossed over to the door. "Jack Powell," he said, extending his hand.

"Kenton Montego," he said, shaking Jack's hand.

"Kenton, it's nice to meet you. We've spoken on the phone. This is my wife, Annie." Jack motioned toward her still on the bed her facing burning up with embarrassment.

"I trust you've found the accommodations good," Kenton said, smiling.

Jack looked over his shoulder toward Annie. Annie nodded fiercely. "We only just got here, but yes, I think everything will be just fine."

"Great. Well, as you know, we live on the property just down the road. There are nice restaurants within walking distance of the villa. Also, within a short jaunt are a couple of very nice wineries, and I'd be happy to set up a wine tasting tour for you. Just ask."

"That all sounds great. So, you say there is a restaurant within walking distance?" Jack glanced at his watch. It was eight o'clock. "We had lunch on the plane, but we could use a bite to eat."

"Yes, a lovely bistro, serving a lighter fare such as paninis, soups, and salads."

"Okay, thanks for the information."

"I'll leave you two to enjoy your accommodations. And please, let us know if we can be of service to you during your stay." Kenton took a few steps backward, turned around, and walked away.

Jack watched him leave and then shut the door. He turned to face Annie with a wide smile broadening on his face.

"That was close. We forgot to close the door," Annie said, snickering.

Jack crossed over to her and held out his hands. Annie pulled up from the bed and slid into his arms. "Let's get out of these traveling clothes and head down to the bistro."

"Why don't you turn on the hot tub so it can be heating up while we're gone?" Annie suggested, motioning toward the garden-style doors that lead to the private portico.

Jack winked. "I'm on it."

THEY DECIDED to walk to the bistro since it was such a gorgeous evening. The wind blew softly across the vine-yards, requiring just a light sweater for Annie. They snuck kisses in as they walked, and within a few minutes they were front and center of a small and very old bistro.

Jack opened the door, and the two entered the dimly lit eatery. It housed only six tables, and all of them were empty.

A young woman looked up from the counter and made eye contact with them. She glanced at her watch and then smiled. "Please have a seat. Anywhere you'd like."

Jack crossed over to a table near the window, pulling out a chair for Annie before he sat down.

The young woman with light brown hair and doe-like brown eyes handed them each a menu. "Something to drink?" she asked.

"Yes, we'd like water and a couple of glasses of wine. What would you suggest?" Jack asked.

"Red or white?"

Jack turned to Annie. "I think I'd like red," Annie said.

"Two glasses of red wine. Something that will help us relax after a long day of traveling," Jack said with a hint of sexiness in his voice that made Annie shiver.

"Do you know what you want to eat?"

Jack glanced down at the menu and surveyed the items. "Oh look, they have wood-fired pizza here. How does that sound?"

"Sounds wonderful," Annie said.

After two glasses of wine and a small pizza, it was

time to head back to the villa. They really picked up the pace as they talked about the warm hot tub and what they wanted to do to each other once they got in it. Between feeling toasty inside from the wine and the magnetic pulses that ran throughout her body, Annie was on fire.

They changed out of their clothes and into the fluffy white robes that hung on hooks in the bathroom and headed to the veranda. The warm glow from the moon was their only light, besides the flicker from a candle on a nearby table. Jack got in first. Annie didn't let her eyes settle in any one place. She pulled in her bottom lip as he helped her in. She slowly eased down to a molded lounge chair. The jets pulsed and streamed, hitting her in all the right places. She leaned back, resting her head on the rim of the tub. "This is so relaxing. We have to have one of these on our property," she said, raising her head slightly, only to drop it back into the tub.

Jack touched her with his foot, causing her to lift her head once more. He rubbed her leg with his foot, and even though it was dark outside, the moon provided just enough light that she could see the burning desire in his eyes. She pulled herself up from her resting spot and joined him on the seat he'd claimed. She found his mouth, slipping her tongue between his lips. He pulled her onto his lap, kissing her hungrily and touching her as he did.

"Either the water is a tad too warm, or you're making me hot," he said under heavy breathing.

She continued kissing him and pulling him closer. "I love you, Jack," she said between kisses.

He pulled away from her, sliding her off his lap. He rose from the steamy water and stepped out, holding his hand out to her. She watched his every movement, shuddering at the thought of them together. She extended her hand to him, and dripping wet, the two entered the villa.

Annie stepped into the tiled bathroom and pulled the two large towels from the rack, tossing one to Jack. He looked at it peculiarly and then tossed it onto the bed. He walked over to her and grabbed the towel she still clenched in her hands and tossed it to the floor. He led her to the big four-poster bed, and Annie not only followed him, but melted in his big strong, loving arms.

CHAPTER 2

The temperature had dropped during the night, making the valley a bit on the cold side. Now the fluffy white robes had a purpose. Snuggled in the deep downy fabric, Jack and Annie sipped on coffee as they looked out onto the vineyards. She drew the cup to her lips and took a sip. "This view is gorgeous."

"Our view is gorgeous, too."

"I know. It's a different kind of gorgeous," Annie said, laughing at their back-and-forth assessment of gorgeous vistas.

"I can't wait to start building," Jack said.

"I know we'll be a bit cramped in my apartment, but it's only for a short while."

Jack furrowed his brows.

"What?" Annie said.

"You do know it will take the better part of a year to build the house, don't you?"

Annie shook her head. "No, I didn't. I guess I thought it would only take a couple of months."

"It might take a contractor that long, but with my job, I'll only be able to devote weekends and vacation time to building it."

Annie drew in another sip of the hot coffee. She picked up the basket of croissants that had been delivered to their room by Kenton's son. She pulled back the checkered cloth and lowered her nose to the baked crescent-shaped bread. "These smell delicious." She took one and then offered Jack the basket.

He plunged his hand into the basket. "Jam?" he asked as he opened the small jar of preserves that Kenton's son said were homemade.

"Yes, please."

"What about hiring someone to help us? Just so it won't take a year to build?" Annie asked as she smothered her croissant with grape jam.

"I'll hire someone to do the electrical and plumbing, but these hands," he said, rotating them back and forth, "are going to build our home board by board."

Annie giggled. "Your motivation and drive are very admirable, dear."

"But ..." Jack said as he took a bite of his breakfast.

"Well … It's just that I think sometimes we can be a bit naïve about how much we are able to do. I include myself in that as well," she said with her eyes all aglow.

"You didn't doubt yourself for a second that Sweet Indulgence would become as profitable as it did, did you?" he asked with half-closed lids and furrowed brows.

Annie reached for the coffee carafe and topped off their cups. "I had my moments. But, yes, you're right. I didn't give up."

"Maybe you should have had more of that backbone when it came to telling your grandmother and auntie to get out of your love life." Jack stared at her intensely.

Annie put her cup down. "Now, just a second, I'm not trying to start an argument here. I was just merely making an observation. Sometimes we do take on more than we can possibly accomplish. It's very commendable, as I said, but I just don't want to be disappointed." Annie shook her head, and a tear appeared on her lower lid.

"I'm sorry, I shouldn't have said that. That was uncalled for. I love your grandmother and auntie, and I know you were only appeasing them because you love them so much."

"Appease them?" Annie raised her voice, but then quickly softened it. "You're right. That's exactly what I was doing. I was going along to get along, but that's all behind us. I found the perfect mate for me, and I love him with all of my heart." She reached out for his hand.

Jack took her hand in his and rubbed her thumb with his. "I'll think about hiring some help. I agree. If I do most of the work, I can still claim that I built it with these two hands." He chuckled.

"That's the spirit. Besides, we have a lot of landscaping to do as well. We really have our work cut out for us."

"As soon as we get back, I'll call some companies," Jack said.

Annie's cell phone vibrated on the table. She glanced over to see the number. It was from her sister, Mary. "I wonder what she wants?" Annie said, picking up the phone. "Hello?"

"I can't believe it. We can't even finish our honeymoon," Annie said as she tossed her clothes into the suitcase.

"I gave our apologies to Kenton and his family. He said if we ever want to come back, he'll allow us to use our unused days."

"That's so nice of him. I hope you told him we will," Annie said, closing her suitcase.

Jack took both suitcases and rolled them toward the door. He glanced around the room. "So long, villa paradise, until next time." He opened the door wide, and he and Annie stepped outside.

They drove to the airport in a daze. Jack didn't mutter a single word about the bakery, but after about half an hour of silence, Annie broke it by sobbing.

"Now, dear, we don't know the damage yet. It could be minimal," Jack said, reassuring her by patting her leg.

"I don't know, Jack. A fire in a kitchen can be devastating."

"Yes, but you have good insurance, and we'll get it all fixed up. I'm just glad no one got hurt."

"Yes, that's a true blessing. All the employees were gone for the day. I wonder what started the fire?"

"We'll find out when we read the report. Right now, why don't you get your camera out and snap some pictures of these spectacular views? The bridge is coming up soon. The sun is shining and it should make a great picture. I'll pull off at the lookout," he said, motioning ahead to the sign indicating the exit.

Annie took pictures of the bridge and of Alcatraz in the distance. She made eye contact with a nice jolly-looking fellow, who seemed to receive the telepathic suggestion she sent him, and offered to take a picture of them both.

Soon they were on their way, once again weaving in and out of traffic in the bay area. Once at the airport, they settled into the leather chairs at their gate, waiting to hear their name. They were on a standby list since they had to make immediate changes to their departure. Annie was stunned and still bewildered by the shocking news that she didn't even hear their names called. Jack went up to the counter, and when he came back, he let her know that everything would be fine. They'd be on the next flight home.

"I WANT to go straight to the bakery," Annie said as they drove into Charleston.

"Okay, but I'm not sure they'll let us in. It might be a crime scene."

Annie cut a strange look at Jack. "A crime scene? Why?"

"Just to determine that the fire wasn't set purposely, I would imagine." Jack turned the car onto the street of the bakery.

Annie's eyes widened when she saw the orange cones and yellow police tape. She gasped. "Oh, my God, look," she said pointing.

Jack pulled the car slowly in front as they both looked at the charred remains of the bakery. Annie began to sob.

"Everything is gone, Jack. The entire bakery is gone." She cupped her face with her hands and cried.

Jack found a parking spot the next block up and pulled the car over. He took a deep breath, letting it out slowly.

Annie wiped her eyes and leaned back into the seat, her head against the headrest. "I can't believe it."

"We don't know that for sure. Right now, it looks pretty bad, but it could just be on the surface. Let's go home and call the authorities and go from there. Let's not get all upset before we have all the answers."

Annie's chest lifted as she took a deep breath. "I have to pick up Buffy from Grandmother's."

"DEAR," Grandmother said, holding out her arms to Annie.

Annie laid her head on her grandmother's shoulder and cried. "It's all gone," she said, muffled by her grandmother's blouse.

Grandmother Lilly held her back and searched her face. "It might be, but you'll rebuild. It's not going to be the end of the world."

Auntie Patty came up behind them and put her arms around them both. "It will be all right, dear, just as Lilly said."

Annie stepped out of their reach and wiped her eyes. "I've cried so darn much these last several hours. We drove by the place, and I just can't believe what I've seen."

"Now, Annie, listen to your grandmother and auntie. It's going to be all right. I think we need to head home now," Jack said, holding Buffy at bay as she tried to lick his face.

Annie took Buffy from Jack and mashed her face into her fur. "Let's go home, Buffy."

"Call us later and let us know how things are," Patty called out.

WITH ONE FOOT in front of the other, Annie crossed to the bedroom in a zombie-like fashion. She plopped down on her bed and stared at the ceiling. Buffy jumped up and lay beside her. Annie turned her head and looked at the fluffy ball. "You know you're not allowed on the bed, girl." Buffy blinked but didn't move a muscle. Annie petted her and continued to look at the ceiling.

Jack came to the room but stopped at the door. He

held up his hands and braced the threshold as he stared into the room. "Baby, why don't you rest a while? I'm going to make some calls and see what I can find out."

"Okay, why don't you do that," she muttered, closing her eyes and soon drifting off to sleep. When she woke, she found Jack next to her, spooning her.

She stretched her arms wide and yawned. "Jack. Jack, wake up," she said as she jostled him with her hands.

He rubbed his eyes and then tried to focus on his watch. "What time is it?"

"We fell asleep." She pitched her legs over the side of the bed and sat upright. She peered at the clock that sat on her end table. "Looks like it's midnight."

"Midnight? We should just keep sleeping then. Why did you wake me up?" He rolled over away from her.

"What did you find out about the bakery?" She was wide awake now.

"I'll tell you in the morning," he mumbled.

"You're going to sleep in your clothes?"

He rolled onto his back and sighed. "I guess not." He tossed his legs over the side of the bed and stood. He unbuttoned his shirt and threw it on the end of the bed. Then he unzipped his pants, stepped out of them, and pitched them near his shirt. Standing in his boxers with his hair sticking up in all directions, he pulled down the bed covers and slid in between the sheets.

Annie watched this play out before her, and within fifteen seconds of him getting into bed, she could hear him softly breathing.

"Men—they can sleep through any disaster."

CHAPTER 3

*a*nnie woke before the sun peeked through the blinds. Her back ached from all her tossing and turning. She stretched and yawned, peering over at Jack as he lay next to her still sleeping. She stood and crossed to the closet, pulling down a light robe from its hanger. She slipped her feet into slippers and shuffled to the kitchen. Coffee—that's what she needed, and plenty of it.

As she reached for the coffee, warm arms embraced her, causing her to twirl around. Her eyes met his. "I didn't even hear you come up behind me." She leaned in to kiss him.

"I'm sneaky like that," he said, kissing her back.

"I couldn't sleep."

"Once you got out of bed, neither could I." He removed his arms and took the single serve coffee pod from her hands. "You sit down and let me get the coffee going."

Annie moved the few steps toward the table and sat down. She watched Jack as he made her coffee first, then his own. She smiled up at him when he placed the mug before her.

"You know … everything is better with coffee."

"I know. I just can't believe we've been hit with this." She held her head in her hands.

"Annie, it's going to be okay. Your insurance will pay for everything. We'll get on the phone, get the police and fire reports, and then make some calls." He sat down across from her and pulled his cup up to his mouth. "Seriously, I promise. It's going to be okay." He drew in a taste of the coffee. "What we really need is some of those delicious cupcakes you make."

Annie began to sob uncontrollably. Jack slid out his chair and ran to her. "Honey, what's wrong? Is it something I said?" He wrapped his arms around her.

"You … you … said cupcakes," she said, her voice muffled by her hands across her mouth.

"Oh, baby, I'm sorry. I didn't mean to upset you. I just thought how nice this cup of coffee would taste with one of your cupcakes." Annie turned toward Jack and buried her face in his chest. He calmly slid his hands up and down her back. "Now, now, honey. Get it all out right here. I love you."

A TRIP to the police department proved to be more upsetting than Jack had promised. It turned out they ruled the fire suspicious, prompting an investigation. Jack read the report three times before giving her the news.

"Now, listen, just because they opened up an investigation doesn't really mean anything," he said, not convincing her.

"Oh, sure, that's what you think, but I think it means someone tried to burn down my bakery on purpose!"

"Why would anyone want to hurt you?" Jack said, cocking his head as he awaited her answer.

"I don't know, competition, maybe?"

"There's room in this city for more than one cupcake bakery. That's ridiculous. You're grasping at straws now."

"I don't know, Jack. I thought about opening up another store nearby. Maybe my inquiry into the leased space prompted this."

Jack sighed. "No, that's crazy talk, Annie. Let's just wait and see what they find out. In the meantime, what do you want to do regarding your business?"

"What do you mean?"

"Do you want to set up somewhere temporarily while we rebuild?"

Annie pursed her lips. "I really hadn't thought about that. I guess that would be a good idea, but where?"

"I have an idea," Jack said. He held out his arms to her. "Come here," he said in a commanding but loving tone that made her march right into his arms. "You know I love you right?"

Annie nodded, her bottom lip protruding.

"You also know that everything is going to be all right. We'll get you set up somewhere, we'll start building our dream home, and yes, it will be stressful, and yes, it will be crazy, but we can handle it. And we can handle it, because why?" Jack pulled away from her and stared into her green eyes.

"Because we love and respect each other." Annie lowered her gaze.

Jack tilted her chin up with one finger. "That's right. And I promised you on our wedding day that I'd take care of you. I don't break my promises." He leaned in and kissed her.

CHAPTER 4

*W*hen Annie called her group of employees together for lunch to discuss how the fire would change things, Betsy's hand flew up first to volunteer.

"We'll need to bake the cupcakes in our homes and then sell them via the truck. I know it's a lot to ask right now, but I'm checking into using a kitchen that is available for lease until the bakery is rebuilt. My sister is going to help, and so are my grandmother and auntie. I've made a schedule for each of you." Annie handed the papers to each employee. "As you can see, this is for your rotation to work the truck. Any questions?"

"I'm ready to help," Rebecca said.

"Me, too," Morgan echoed.

Nodding his head, Peter raised his hand. "Boss, you can count me in."

Annie smiled. "Thank you, Peter. Thank you, everyone, this means so much to me. So Friday night will be our first test run, and Betsy and I will be the guinea pigs. Saturday it will be me and Rebecca. Rebecca will also be helping her folks with their truck, so she'll be bouncing back and forth. That should be interesting," Annie said, heaving her shoulders up.

"Why don't I take Rebecca's spot for Saturday?" Peter suggested.

"I thought you might be working for Jack on Saturday. But if you can switch with Rebecca that would be awesome."

"Consider it done. I can ask Jack to put me on the schedule for Sunday."

"Great, sounds like we have a plan. Thank you for sticking with me as we get through this ordeal together. Jack seems to think it won't take long to rebuild Sweet Indulgence. I hope he's right. Enjoy your lunch," Annie said as her eyes traveled to everyone's plates that now sat before them. "But before we do enjoy our lunch, let's just say a little blessing, shall we?"

Everyone bowed their heads as Annie shared her thoughts about the recent fire and how blessed she felt that none of her employees had been hurt.

ANNIE BLEW the hair out of her eyes that kept escaping from under her hairnet. She reached into the hot oven and withdrew the next tin of baked cupcakes and set them on the wire rack to cool. She did a count, mumbling the numbers.

Her tiny kitchen soon had stacks of baked cupcakes ready to be iced. She dropped down on her couch, apron and all, and propped her feet up on the coffee table. Her eyes made contact with Buffy's. "I know, you need a walk, but I just need a break right now. Can you just hold it, please?"

Buffy cocked her head and then ran over to Annie. Annie leaned over and grunted as she rubbed her head. "My feet are killing me. I've baked six dozen cupcakes so far."

The phone rang just then. Annie recognized the number. "Hello, Mary. How are you?"

"I'm up to my neck in cupcakes, that's how I'm doing. How about you?"

"The same. I just sat down. This is the first time I took a break all day. I'm exhausted."

"I told Grandmother and Auntie to go take a nap. They've been at it for a few hours. Now it's my turn."

"I'm sorry to have saddled you with so much, but you

guys have the larger kitchen."

"I know, no worries. Have you talked to Betsy today?"

"No, I haven't. I suppose no news is good news."

"Or she's lying dead in the kitchen from exhaustion."

"Mary McPherson! What an awful thing to say."

"Well, I didn't mean anything by it. But she had a lot to do as well."

Annie's mind wandered to a vision of Betsy lying on the floor, covered in flour. "Listen, I better go. I'll be over later to help frost." Annie clicked the phone off and searched for Betsy's number. A sigh of relief escaped her lips when she heard her voice. "How are you doing, Betsy?"

"I'm doing all right. I have three more dozen to make then I'll be icing them."

"Okay, I'm about done here for the day. I'll be heading over to help Mary ice the ones they baked today."

"Okay, what time are you coming over on Friday?"

"By about two o'clock. We rented a van that is an empty shell inside and I also rented some baking racks and pans so we should be able to load the cupcakes easily. Anything that won't fit we can just transport in our own vehicles. We should be ready to sell by five o'clock."

"Okay, I'll be ready and so will the ten dozen cupcakes," Betsy said with a giggle.

Annie furrowed her brows and became silent.

"Annie? Are you there?" Betsy asked.

"Yes, I'm here. It's just when you said ten dozen and I know I did six, and I think Mary, Grandmother, and Auntie did ten, too, it puts it in perspective the number of cupcakes we're dealing with."

"Yes, it's a lot, considering the short time we had and the space to do them in. I miss the big kitchen and plentiful countertops, not to mention the storage space the bakery offered," Betsy said.

"Well, it is what it is. That's Jack's famous saying. We'll make it work. See you on Friday." Annie clicked the phone off and leaned back on the sofa.

Buffy let out a loud bark.

"No rest for the weary, huh, Buffy?" Annie rose from the couch and crossed over to where her leash hung. "Okay, but it has to be quick. I have cupcakes to frost."

After the short walk outside, Annie resumed her baking detail. She whipped up a batch each of cream cheese, chocolate, and plain vanilla frosting. She'd just put the finishing touches on the vanilla frosted cupcakes when Jack came home.

"I hope you'll be fine with toast and cereal for dinner. I'm pooped," Annie said with slumped shoulders.

"Baby, we can go out to eat," Jack said, embracing her. He wiped some frosting off of her cheek and tasted it. "Cream cheese?"

Annie tried to smile. "Cream cheese, chocolate, and vanilla. I'm too tired to go out to eat. Besides, I have to go over and help frost cupcakes at Grandmother's."

Jack crossed toward the bedroom, taking his jacket off. "I can help. Why don't we go over together and frost cupcakes?" He turned around, winking at her.

Annie couldn't help but smile. In all of her exhaustion, just seeing Jack's glowing face and glistening eyes put a spark in her. She untied her apron and tossed it on the table.

She traveled toward the bedroom where she found Jack slowly undressing. He'd taken off his shoes, loosened his tie, and as she watched him remove the belt from his pants, deep feelings began to stir inside. He turned toward her as he began to unbutton his pants.

"I'll just change, and we can eat something light, and I'll be ready to help."

Annie moved toward him.

Jack's eyes met hers. "What are you doing?" he asked as she embraced him with her arms around his waist.

"I'm not *that* exhausted." She pulled his mouth down to meet hers.

CHAPTER 5

*F*riday night at the food truck event, proved to be successful with a decent stream of customers, more indicative of young professionals winding down after a busy week at the office, with a few different scenarios throw in, and totally manageable. But Saturday was a whole other ball game. The sun was out, the temperature perfect, and that brought droves of people to not just the cupcake truck, but all the food trucks. Every spare inch of the picnic table benches was taken by a body, and many more stood around holding their paper bowls and plates with various items such as mac and cheese with pulled pork atop, lumpia and fried rice and of course, cupcakes.

Annie did a quick survey of the trays. "We have about two dozen left. This is crazy!"

Peter took a plastic serving glove from the box and put it on. He handed a cupcake to a young lady that had that starry-eyed look. Annie watched as she flirted with him; he was totally oblivious to her subtle come-on.

By four o'clock they were sold out. Annie began to clean up inside the truck and wait for Jack. "Peter, help me put the flap down," Annie said, taking the long pole and hooking it for ease to lower the door.

"I'M GOING to park the truck in our lot," Jack said, jumping in the driver's seat.

"I'll follow you," Annie said, touching his arm that rested on the outside of the door.

Annie pulled in right behind Jack and barely had put the car in park when Peter jumped out. Annie lowered the window down. "Thanks for helping me today, Peter."

Peter took a step toward the window and leaned in. "Hey, no worries. Glad to help."

Annie watched as he jogged up to Jack. They laughed and then Jack playfully swatted Peter's arm. Peter returned the jab, and it went on like that for a bit. Annie smiled. Jack was great around kids.

Jack opened the car door and slid into the passenger seat. "I'm usually the driver, this feels odd." He lowered his head onto the headrest, turning slightly and smiled. "But I could get used to it." He pulled his head forward. "Hey, so Peter said you guys really had a lot of customers. That's good, right?"

"Yes, it is, but what a lot of work. I think we may have to come up with something different," she said.

Jack brushed his hand across his chin. "What do you mean?"

"I don't know exactly, but I can't have Mary, Grandmother, Auntie, and Betsy all baking cupcakes each week. Mary has another job, remember?"

"Yes, I do, and tourism is about to get into full swing here, and she'll be busy with Diane, soon."

"Yep, and I have to consider Betsy. She retired once before from the baking business. I know she helped at Sweet Indulgence, but she had a big kitchen to work in."

"This is just temporary. By the way, I heard back from the insurance company."

Annie widened her eyes in anticipation of Jack's next words. "Okay … what did they say?"

"They are going to issue a check by next week, so you can start rebuilding. They suggested you start getting bids. Man, I wish I wasn't going to be so busy with the new house. I'd love to help you."

"I know," she said, patting his hand. "But you do have

your hands full. I'm sure I can find some talented construction workers in this town."

"I also have some other good news," Jack said, a smile spreading across his face.

Annie lifted her brows. "Do tell."

"The bookstore next door to the cupcakery—"

"The one owned by old man Johnson?" Annie said, interrupting him.

Jack tipped his head. "He fell down a flight of stairs at his home and broke his hip."

Annie gasped.

"He's going to be okay, but his family convinced him it was time to give up the store. They'll be clearing out the place, and it will be up for lease soon. I ran into his daughter. She told me everything."

Annie cocked her head. "You know his daughter? You never told me that."

Jack fiddled with a string on his shirt.

"Oh, I see. You *KNEW* his daughter. As in dated her?"

"It was just once. We weren't compatible at all. She smelled like musty old books," Jack said laughingly.

Annie laughed. "Well, that is good news, because I could expand the bakery!"

"That's what I thought. You might as well knock out

some walls while you rebuild. You could make it a true café. I even thought you might consider expanding the menu."

Annie turned her body so her back was now up against the door. She placed her hands on her lap. "How do you mean?"

"Well, you have Betsy Walker who is an excellent baker."

"Like wedding cakes?" Annie said, twisting her mouth.

"Nah, I was thinking more along the lines of cookies. Cupcakes and cookies go together, right?"

Annie studied his eyes. They pulled her right in, making it difficult to focus. "I like it. We could have fancy coffee, too—cappuccino's, lattes, and hot chocolates."

Jack lifted his body and moved a few spaces to the left toward her. He reached out and took her hands in his. "I like the way you think."

"Oh, Jack, I have so many ideas swimming in my head right now. Do I want black and white tiles, chrome tables and chairs, or maybe a more country feel with wood floors and benches? I don't know, the ideas are endless. And we'll be pet-friendly, so how about we have homemade pet treats for sale, too?"

Jack raised his brows. "Now, that's the best idea so far." He leaned in for a kiss, not quite close enough to meet her mouth. She played hard to get and then at the last moment he pulled her in and met her mouth.

CHAPTER 6

She'd just come back from an exhausting visit with her grandmother and auntie. All she could think about was putting her feet up and sharing a glass of wine with Jack. After she walked Buffy, that is.

Annie shut the door, her eyes drifting to the couch where Jack sat. On the coffee table, where she'd envisioned propping her feet, sat some sort of diagram. As she crossed over to the area, she recognized them to be house plans.

"Hi, dear," she said, leaning over and kissing him on the forehead.

Jack mumbled a greeting. He pushed back, resting his head on the back of the couch. "House plans," he said, motioning with his chin.

"I see that," she said, dropping down next to him. "I

was going to prop my tired feet right there," she said laughingly. Buffy let out a bark and came running toward the couch, jumping right on her lap. "Hey, girl," she said, nuzzling her neck.

"I took her for her walk already," Jack said, leaning forward again as he studied the plans.

"Thank you! How'd you know I would be exhausted?"

"You went to your grandmother's." He wrapped his arms around her and squeezed her tightly.

"You're the best. It was a very exhausting visit. Grandmother wanted to know how much longer until the bakery was rebuilt. Auntie wanted to know when we could get together for dinner again. It went on and on."

Jack knitted his brows together. "Did you tell them they just started on the remodeling?"

"I did," she said, slipping her shoes off and pulling her legs up on the couch. She carefully moved Buffy between them.

Jack reached over and patted Buffy on the head. "These things take time. Rome wasn't built in a day."

Annie cocked her head. "Jack, they're old."

"And impatient. Let's talk about our house. This is what I've been pondering for the last fifteen or twenty minutes." He ran his finger along the square boxes. "This is our bedroom with an adjacent bathroom. Do you think the linen closet should be here, or do you want me to move it over here?" He pointed his finger into another area.

"I like it where you have it. It's very convenient to get towels and stuff."

"Okay, it will be left as is, then. What's for dinner?" he asked, grinning from ear to ear.

"I don't know. Where would you like to go?" she said, teasing him.

"Oh, I get it. The honeymoon is over with. No cooking dinners for me."

"No, I'm just being silly. I know we have a box of cereal in the cabinet." She winked and then leaned in and kissed him.

"Not cereal again. Put your shoes back on, we're going out." He folded the plans at the creases and put them into the folder lying next to them.

"We had an invite over at Grandmother's, but I just couldn't take any more interrogations."

Jack stood and reached over, pulling Buffy into his arms. "Let's go to the taco place. We can take Buffy, too."

ANNIE LICKED the salt off of the rim then put the glass to

her lips, taking in the taste of the lime drink. She licked her lips and sighed. "This—this is what I so needed tonight."

Jack peered over the plastic-coated menu. "I can't decide between the cheese enchilada dinner and the taco salad." He laid the menu down and picked up his margarita.

The server came up to the table to take their orders. Annie went first, since she'd already decided on the tamales. Jack ended up getting the enchilada dinner. Annie looked over Jack's shoulder, only to see a familiar face. The person went out of their way to be recognized, waving their hands all over. "Oh, look, it's Rebecca ..." Her eyes traveled to the person sitting next to her. "And Michael!"

"Michael who," Jack said, twisting around. He raised his hand and waved then turned back around. "Oh, that Michael, I guess they're an item now?"

"This is sort of awkward." Annie lowered her mouth to the straw and drew in some more of her drink.

"Not really. She's old enough to date," Jack said, dipping a tortilla chip in the bowl of salsa.

Annie pursed her mouth and tapped her fingers on the table.

"You aren't jealous, are you?" Jack said, smiling.

"Jealous! Who me?" She reached across the table and

dipped a chip, dripping salsa as she brought it to her mouth. She crunched the chip and swallowed. "I'm married to you. Why would I be jealous?"

"I wondered if you'd figure that part out." Jack leaned back in his chair, brushing his hand across his chin.

"Oh, Jack, I'm sorry. Of course, I'm not jealous. But it's kind of weird that my employee is dating my old boyfriend."

"Things like this happen every day. It's no biggie."

"I guess. Anyway, I'm happy for her, I really am. There aren't too many people who work as hard as she does. She deserves happiness."

Between the slurping of margaritas and crunching of chips, Jack and Annie mostly ate in silence. Annie looked up just in time to see Rebecca and Michael moving their way.

"Hey, Annie," Rebecca said, touching her lightly on the shoulder.

"Rebecca! Glad to see you out. I know days off for you are a rarity."

Rebecca gazed up at Michael. He wrapped his arm around her shoulder and pulled her close.

"And of course, you, too, Michael. I'm sure you really appreciate when you can get away from the hospital."

Michael tipped his head. "It's nice to see you guys, too. How was the honeymoon?"

"Cut short," Jack said, interjecting.

"Oh, yeah, the fire, I'm so sorry about that. But Rebecca tells me you're rebuilding and expanding."

"Yes, we're going to expand into the old bookstore space. I hope I can keep Rebecca on. Her customer service is top-notch."

Michael smiled. "Well, hon, we should be going." He made eye contact with Annie.

Annie slouched a bit before answering. "Take care, guys."

Annie could feel Jack boring holes into her.

"What?"

"You are pathetic. Why did you talk like you'd lost your best friend, or more like you just broke up with Michael yourself?"

"Did I sound sad?"

"Sad, mad, depressed, I don't know, but it was clearly obvious. I hope Rebecca didn't see that."

"Oh, geez, I really don't know what got into me. I couldn't care less who he dates. If they are happy together, that's all that matters."

"Right! So maybe the next time you see them together, you'll convey that instead of the pathetic schoolgirl routine." Jack took another bite of his dinner.

A tear rolled down Annie's face. "I'm sorry, Jack. I think I've been through quite a bit of stuff lately. I planned a wedding, went on a honeymoon, which was cut short to come back to a burned-out business, and am now trying to rebuild, and not to mention, build a home."

Jack tightened his lips. He reached out and cupped her hands with his. "Apology accepted. I know you don't really care about him. How could you, when you're married to a guy like me?" He said, winking at her.

Annie squeezed his hands and chuckled. "Not to mention, all the moves you have in the *ahem* … bedroom."

CHAPTER 7

"Okay, close your eyes," Jack said, helping her out of the boat.

"Jack, I'm scared. I can't see."

"I'm right here. Just take one step after another."

Holding on to him tightly, she did as he instructed her. It didn't take a rocket scientist to figure out that he'd taken her to the island to show her the progress.

"Okay, just a little further," Jack said, guiding her with his voice.

"I'm so excited," she said in a high-pitched voice.

"Okay, open your eyes," he said, right after they quickly came to a stop.

Annie opened her eyes and stared straight ahead. Her hand flew to her mouth. "Oh, wow, I had no idea you'd be this far along in the construction." She ran closer toward the house.

"Be careful! It's a construction site, with nails and other debris," he said, calling out to her as he tried to catch up.

Annie climbed the steps and stepped into the framed area. She twirled around. "This is the front entrance, correct?"

Jack led the way through the maze of lumber. He called out each room as they passed in between studs holding up the frame. "This is the master bedroom."

Annie ran into his arms and squeezed him tightly. "I love you, Jack. This is our house. This is our bedroom."

Jack reared his head back and laughed. "I know. It's starting to look like a house."

Annie ran out of the room toward the back of the house. She looked up and around. "What room is this? I don't recall this being in the house plans."

Jack came up behind her and cradled her waist in his arms. "A sunroom."

Annie spun around and faced him. "A sunroom?" She leaned in and kissed him.

"I figured a house with a big front porch to see the gorgeous water views also needed a sunroom to look out at the beautiful back parcel and the gorgeous greenery and landscaping we have. Not to mention the marsh area."

"We'll see all kinds of wildlife," Annie said, her eyes twinkling.

"The crew is estimating the house should be done by Labor Day."

"That's awesome. The construction crew at the bakery told me today they should be done by the Fourth of July."

"That's fabulous." Jack pulled her in close. "I love you, Mrs. Powell." He leaned in and found her warm mouth, tracing her lips with his tongue, urging her to respond. She let out a small groan. She pushed against his strong frame, kissing him with all the passion she could muster, enjoying the sweet depths of his mouth. His hands began to roam her body, which almost brought her to her knees, pulling him down with her. She stopped the kiss and stepped back, smoothing down her hair and clothes.

"Wow, that was some kiss."

Jack stepped toward her, taking her hands into his. "You know I love you so much. You drive me wild with passion."

"I'm having a hard time not taking you right here and now ... in the sunroom," she said, her breathing clearly labored.

"I won't complain if you do," he said, pulling her close.

ANNIE HELD on to Jack's strong arms as he tried to steer the boat into the designated slip at the dock. "Honey, I'm trying to park the boat," he said, stealing a quick kiss.

A throaty sound came out of her mouth. "I know, baby, but I love you," she said, pulling him toward her.

Jack lifted her chin with his finger. "Baby, stop. I know you're hungry for me, but let's wait until I get you home."

"Hurry up. That little taste of you out at Sweet Magnolia is driving me wild. I want more."

Jack's eyes widened. "I'm hurrying. You wouldn't want me to wreck the boat, would you?"

SATISFIED, but exhausted, the two pulled the sheets up to just under their chins, their heads slightly propped against the headboard. Annie dared not look his way. She'd been a wild animal in bed. She felt him move toward her.

"Okay, that was utterly intense. I have one thing to ask you," Jack said, whispering in her ear.

Annie rolled her head sideways, focusing on his deep and longing look. "What's that?" she said, fighting to keep her voice steady.

"That we never lose this chemistry. I want us getting our groove on, even when we're seventy years old." He pulled up and kissed her on the cheek.

A slow grin quirked her mouth. "Oh, you can count on it," she said, rolling over and straddling him.

A smirk sprang to his mouth. "That's what I'm talking about," he said, claiming her mouth.

CHAPTER 8

*O*ver the course of thirty days, transformations of both Sweet Magnolia and Sweet Indulgence took place. Meeting deadlines regarding the house and business kept them hopping, and most nights they fell into bed from sheer exhaustion. She, along with her employees, kept the food truck idea afloat and sold cupcakes, but it wasn't the same. Less and less of her repeat customers came around, but thankfully young people living on campus nearby were becoming the new regulars, and if everything went according to plan, they'd become repeat customers once Sweet Indulgence opened its doors again.

Shopping for contents for the bakery became the number one thing on Annie's list to accomplish. Jack insisted she take Mary along. He had his hands full with contractors who weren't following instructions. Diane, Jack's sister, gave Mary the day off so she could accompany her. They headed off to the big home warehouse for some inspiration.

"I love these old crates. How could you use them at the bakery?" Mary asked, running her hand along the old wooden boxes.

"I don't know, but they are cute," Annie said. "Oh, look at this, Mary." Annie picked up embroidered pillows with cupcakes on them.

"And look over there, a bench." Mary giggled as she tore across the room to sit on it.

"That would look so cute out in front," Annie said.

"I can't wait to see it put together. It will be the chicest café slash bakery Charleston ever had!"

Annie hugged Mary. "Thanks for the vote of confidence, and for coming with me today. By the way … how are you and Danny doing?"

A wide grin shot across Mary's mouth. "We're doing good! He makes me happy. We just take each day as it comes."

"Is it serious, though?"

"I don't really know. I just know we can't go very long without seeing each other or at least hearing each other's voice."

"I'd say that's pretty serious. Have you been to Grandmother's for dinner with him lately?"

Mary shook her head. "No, why?"

"They've been bugging me to bring Jack over. We're just dead tired each night, and going over there is not high on our priority list. I figured since you lived there, they saw you two often."

"I'm over at Danny's place a lot. I sneak in when they're fast asleep, snoring, and with their sleep masks on." Mary laughed out loud and then quickly covered her mouth.

Annie looked around the store to see if anyone looked their way. "Mary, *shh*, but I hear you. But a little voice inside my head tells me they won't be around forever, and I should make time to go see them."

Mary pulled her bottom lip and bit down.

"Anyway, I'll figure it out. Let's purchase some of these items and go have lunch."

"OKAY, JUST FOLLOW MY LEAD," Annie said, knocking on the door.

Shuffling sounds came from the other side and soon the door flew open. Grandmother Lilly's mouth dropped open. "Annie!"

"Hello, Grandmother." Annie stepped inside.

"And Jack, too!" Grandmother said, hugging first Annie then Jack. "What brings you two here?"

Annie lifted the casserole dish. "Dinner."

"You brought us dinner? Patty! Annie and Jack are here," she said as she shuffled toward the main living area.

Annie gently bumped shoulders with Jack. "I told you they'd be excited to see us."

"Oh, my, it's Annie and Jack," Patty said as she tried to pull herself up out of the chair. "I was just resting my eyes."

"*Humph.* More like snoozing," Lilly said.

"We brought dinner, so you two just sit back and relax. Give us a few minutes to get the table set, and we'll call you." Annie marched into the kitchen with Jack following behind.

Annie set the casserole dish on the counter and took the basket of rolls from Jack. She opened the cabinet overhead and handed him four plates. "The silverware is over in that drawer," she said, motioning with her chin. She turned on the oven and popped both the casserole dish and the tray of rolls into the oven. They just needed reheating. She opened the fridge. Her eyes widened when she saw the empty shelves. "Jack, look in here. What do you see?"

"A stick of butter, a jar of blackberry preserves, a—"

"Exactly," she said, not letting him finish. "It's empty —no food."

Jack pulled his head back out of the fridge and stood. "I thought Mary was keeping an eye on things here."

"Apparently not. I think she's too wrapped up in your cousin."

"Now, just a second, I'm not sure I like the way you said cousin."

"Well, it's true. She's spending a lot of time with him, only to sneak in here after they're asleep."

"If you know that, then why wouldn't you put a stop to that?" Jack tilted his head as he furrowed his brows.

"I just discovered it when she and I went shopping. But I guess I didn't put the two together as far as her not making sure things are done around here. That's part of the stipulation of her living here for free."

"What are you going to do?"

"I'll casually ask them both tonight how things are really going. I must have all the facts before I lower the boom on Mary."

"She'll probably move out," Jack said, leaning up against the counter.

"I don't know, Jack. This could present a problem for us, especially after we move out to the island."

Jack stood, nodding.

The timer went off on the oven, signaling the casserole was heated through. Annie pulled out the oven mitts and then removed the hot dish. She carried it into the dining area. "Grab a trivet for me, Jack. It's in the bottom drawer nearest the oven."

Jack quickly retrieved the trivet and moved in front of her, beating her to the table. "I'll get the rolls," he said, backing away from the table.

"Grandmother and Auntie, dinner is ready."

Jack helped Grandmother and Annie helped Patty. For the first time in several months, she realized how much they'd aged. It seemed like just yesterday they were attending bridge parties and working their magic, trying to set her up on blind dates. Now, shuffling around, dozing in chairs, and apparently not eating much, was their norm.

"This is delicious, Annie," Grandmother said.

"Agreed, we've not had a home-cooked meal in months," Patty chimed in.

"I thought Mary was tending to your meals," Annie said softly.

"She tries, but she's with Danny a lot and doesn't get home until quite late," Lilly said.

"It might be time to think about different living arrangements," Annie said, looking at Lilly first then Patty.

Lilly put her fork down. "What do you mean? Like moving to an old folks' home?"

"No, of course not."

Lilly tilted her head and strummed her fingers on the table. "Well, then, what?"

Annie glanced over at Jack. He'd just put a bite in his mouth. He chewed it quickly, wiping his mouth with a napkin. "Maybe we could hire someone to come in once in a while."

"A stranger?" Patty asked skeptically.

"They'd be vetted, by a company," Jack said, stumbling over his words.

"A glorified babysitter," Lilly said, squaring her shoulders.

"Okay, let's not get worked up over this. We'll think about it. That means you both think about alternatives, as well. Jack and I will be living on the island in a couple of months. I don't know how much we can count on Mary. Things are changing for all of us," Annie said, lowering her eyes to her plate.

"You speak like we have one foot in the grave! That's the furthest thing from the truth. We're alive, vibrant, and clearly capable of living on our own," Lilly said, obviously rattled by their current discussion.

"Okay, Grandmother, I hear you. Let's just finish our dinner. Jack and I have a surprise for you guys."

Both Grandmother and Auntie's eyebrows raised.

"I love surprises," Auntie Patty said, gobbling her food.

"Auntie, take your time, please. We can't have anyone getting indigestion tonight," Annie said shaking her head.

"Indigestion? What about choking?" Grandmother said with a scowl. "I doubt seriously that Jack would enjoy performing the Heimlich maneuver tonight." She grunted then scooped some vegetables on her spoon.

Jack tipped his head. "You have a point, Lilly, you have a point."

JACK AND ANNIE quickly washed the dishes and cleaned up the kitchen. They were trying to beat the clock and Grandmother's and Auntie's bedtime. Soon they'd be yawing, and well, it wouldn't be a pretty sight, Annie knew first hand. There were dentures to brush, faces to slather night cream on, and more. The nightly routine these two old women performed was enough to put grey hair on Annie's head.

Getting them into the car was always a challenge. Jack opened the doors wide and took Lilly's arm. She slowly stepped down and then turned her body slightly plopping suddenly to the seat. Jack's body halfway inside the car, he helped with the seatbelt. Meanwhile, Annie was on the other side helping Auntie Patty.

"Auntie, slide in, keep your legs out here and then slowly move them inside," Annie said.

"Annie, I can handle getting into a car, thank you."

"Auntie," Annie said.

"I'm sorry, child. I didn't mean to bite your head off. I know you're only helping."

Patty picked up her legs and slid them inside.

"Can you manage the seatbelt?" Annie asked crossing her arms.

"If you would be a dear…"

Annie leaned inside and assisted with the seatbelt.

"And we're off," she said as she ran around the car and passed Jack going to the driver's side.

They stood a moment gazing at one another from the car roof. Then Jack tapped the roof with his fingers. "Ready?" He smiled.

"Ready as I'll ever be," she said flashing a smile.

"Okay, Grandmother, take Jack's arm."

Annie stuck her arm out for Patty. "Do you realize where you're at?"

Patty pulled her lids half closed and squinted. "I don't know exactly."

"Sweet Indulgence. We're at the bakery!" Annie gently pulled Patty along toward the front door.

"Is it done?" Lilly said.

"Almost, Grandmother." Annie put the key in the door and opened it wide. She flicked on the light and waited for Jack to catch up with Lilly.

"Oh, my word, it's so light and bright in here," Lilly said.

"It feels brighter because it's still an empty space. But after we get the tables and chairs in here and the artwork on the walls, it will warm it up quite a bit. But take a look at our display case. It's double the size we used to have," Annie said, leading Patty deeper into the space.

"I just love the wood floors. But is that really smart with food and drink?" Patty said.

"These are a new product on the market made out of bamboo. They are waterproof, natural, and I just fell in love with them when the salesman showed them to me."

"What color are the walls?" Lilly said.

"It's called butterscotch. I think it really looks nice and will look great with the furniture."

"When will it be completely done and open for business? Are you going to have a grand opening?" Lilly asked.

Annie tossed her head back and chuckled. "One question at a time, Grandmother. It should be finished in about two weeks. They're working on the kitchen, putting in the appliances and countertops. The furniture is scheduled for delivery on June thirtieth. As for a grand opening, Jack and I thought a grand re-opening would be suitable. Morgan and Rebecca are making flyers, and Betsy is creating a cupcake and cookie just for the re-opening. I have no idea what they are, they'll be a surprise."

"I'd like to come on that day and have a special cookie and a fancy cup of coffee," Patty said shyly.

Annie pulled Patty in closer. "Of course, Auntie, I'll make sure you both are part of the celebration."

Annie looked up in time to see Lilly pulling Jack around the café. She could hear her tell him how she thought things should be decorated. Jack went along with whatever she suggested. He knew it would be much easier to just go along with her.

Once Patty realized her sister was out of earshot, she took the opportunity to talk to Annie. "I know you're worried and concerned about us, but you shouldn't be. I'm more than capable of taking care of Lilly."

Annie tightened her brows together. "I just want what is best for you both."

"I think what we need is to get out a bit more. We sit in that house day after day, no visitors, nothing to look forward to. Just coming out here tonight has put a jump in my step. I probably won't be able to fall asleep tonight."

Annie lowered her chin and studied Patty's face. "That is probably because you had coffee with your dinner, Auntie."

Auntie brushed her hand across Annie's arm. "Silly girl, that's not why. It's because we got to see you guys tonight. And we're just so happy you found the time."

Annie drew in a deep breath. They'd noticed. They truly noticed she'd not been around much, since she'd met Jack really. And now that she was married, they saw even less of her.

"I know, Auntie. I promise to do better about visiting."

Jack's and Lilly's voices grew louder as they finished making the rounds of the café and came back to them.

"That kitchen is huge, Patty," Lilly said, puffing out her chest.

"Well, we better get you guys back home. It's getting late."

"Promise us you won't forget to bring us here for the big celebration, Annie," Patty said.

Annie softened her voice. "I promise."

"By the way, what was ever decided regarding the fire? Was it set on purpose?" Lilly inquired.

"It was determined that a short in the wiring for the

dishwasher, of all things, started it. They ruled it an accident," Annie said.

"What a relief. The thought of someone setting the fire on purpose disturbed me," Patty said.

"Me, too," Annie said.

CHAPTER 9

*A*lmost asleep, Jack startled Annie when he rose out of bed and shook her. "I have the perfect solution."

Annie opened her eyes wide, her heart beating a mile a minute. She rolled her head to the side and peered at Jack with half-crazed eyes. "What are you talking about? You woke me up!"

"I know the perfect solution to our problem with Lilly and Patty."

Annie scooted up on the bed and rested her head against the headboard. "What issue with Lilly and Patty?"

"The one that we're faced with regarding their age and care." Jack stuck his neck out and blinked a few times.

Annie sighed. "I have a solution to that. I'm going … or rather, we are going to visit more often."

"What if I suggested they move in with us?" Jack said without any hesitation.

"Jack! We have a one-bedroom apartment. Buffy is even feeling the squeeze since you moved in."

Jack pursed his lips. "No, I mean at Sweet Magnolia."

Annie's eyes roamed his entire face, studying him hard. She knew he must be joking and soon he'd let out a big laugh to let her know. But the laugh never came. "You're serious?"

"Yes, I am. They only have you … and Mary. My grandparents have so many people looking in on them. Lilly and Patty, well, they're kind of alone."

Annie brushed the hair back from her face and sighed. "True, but they are so different from your elder family. They've always wanted to be independent."

"Just think about it. We have plenty of room on the land to build a nice granny-size unit. That way they'll still maintain some independence," Jack said.

"What about Mary?"

Jack brushed his hand across his chin. "Good point. Maybe it's time for her to get her own place?"

"Grandmother would never sell that house. She insists it's to be passed down to Mary and me. I don't have the heart to tell her, but I don't really want it. I don't think Mary does either."

"It's been in your family for generations, Annie. It's hard to let go of a piece of history such as that. It would be like selling off our land to someone. I could never do that."

Annie puckered her lips. "I need to think this through and figure out what the best solution will be for all of us," Annie said as she slid back down into bed, pulling the sheets up.

"Good night," Jack said, turning off the light.

She'd just closed her eyes when a thought popped into her head. Her eyes flew open, and she bolted straight up. "I have it!" She reached up and turned on the bedside lamp.

Jack, blinded by the sudden light, blinked a few times.

"I have it. I have the solution," Annie said, pushing him playfully.

"Okay," he said, drawing out the word groggily.

"We'll build the granny unit and slowly get them used to the idea. We'll encourage them to stay the night after dinners and family events. Eventually, they'll just move in permanently. What do you think? Do you think they'll buy it?"

"I think it might work. But what about making sure they are taken care of properly while they do reside in the grand palace," Jack said smirking.

"Mary is going to have to do a better job. I'll insist on it. I think I'm going to reach out to one of those agencies as well. I'll start off by having someone come by once a week and see how that goes."

"You heard what they said about strangers in their house," Jack reminded her.

"Well, let me work on that. I know how to get around those two old ladies. I've been doing it for years." Annie leaned over and kissed Jack's cheek.

"Okay, so I'll have plans drafted up for a nice cottage-style unit, with two bedrooms and a large bathroom in the middle. Sort of like the Jack and Jill setup we're doing with the kids' bedrooms."

A warm smile crossed her face. "Like the kids' rooms? That's what you're calling the upstairs area?"

He held her eyes with his. "We are going to have children, right? And they are going to have the bedrooms upstairs, right?"

"Yes, Jack, we are. It just hit me differently when I heard the words come out of your mouth. When the time is right, we're going to have babies—and lots of them." She found his mouth and kissed him long, tasting every sweet nuance of him.

He placed his hands on her and moved her back. "Lots of babies?"

Annie burst into a smile.

"I better add another bedroom to the plan, then."

CHAPTER 10

*A*nnie pulled into the parking lot, taking a moment to gather her thoughts. The lady on the phone had sounded so nice and had put her at ease, but this was a very delicate situation, and Annie didn't want to blow it. Grandmother and Auntie would never forgive her.

"Thank you for meeting me," Annie said, extending her hand to the smiling woman.

"Of course." She motioned for Annie to take a seat.

"As I mentioned on the phone, I have a grandmother and auntie who are in their late seventies, living together in a large old home down near the waterfront. My sister lives there too, but she's very busy with work and life, and so I'm afraid things are not as they should be. I'm dealing with my sister as well, but I thought another set of eyes on the situation would be good."

"Absolutely. It's very hard for the older generation to accept they need help, so having someone come in and visit is a good way to break the ice."

Annie rocked her head up and down. "I agree. So, what exactly do you propose?"

"Instead of sending someone too young, we send someone in their age bracket, around ten years younger, that can just go over and maybe offer to take them out to lunch or to the store. How does that sound?"

"Sounds wonderful. They still like to putter around in the kitchen, but I'm getting concerned about that as well."

"It sounds like money is not an issue, correct?" the lady inquired.

Annie shook her head.

"There are some great meal delivery services available, some even make gourmet foods. How about we set something up on a trial basis and see if they like the food?"

"That's a great idea. I'll give them a hint it's going to happen so they can prepare," Annie said.

"Often times, it's best to convince them that they are helping the visitor out and not emphasize that they are there to help them. It helps bring those walls down that you or anyone is trying to take their independence away."

"Oh, that's good. My grandmother and auntie love to play bridge. They belonged to a club, but since I got married and Mary is busy, I don't think they are getting there much."

"See? That's exactly what I need to know in order to pair them up with someone just right. What other interests do they have?"

"They love to go to musicals at the performing arts center and have lunch out. They enjoy going to the park and watching children and dogs play. They indulge in wine and scotch after dinner…"

The woman looked up from jotting the items down. "It's probably not a good idea for them to drink while they're alone."

Annie twisted her mouth to the side and then lowered her eyes. "I'll work on that," she whispered.

"I'll put all of this information into our database and find the perfect person or persons to help. Give me about ten minutes."

Annie glanced at her watch. "I'm going to step outside and make a phone call. I'll be right back."

Once outside, Annie held the phone to her ear, listening to the rings until Mary's voice came on.

"Hey, Sis, what's up?"

Annie quickly gave her the rundown of what she was up to.

"Okay, sounds great. I hope you can pull the wool over their eyes. They're pretty smart," Mary said.

"It's not me, it's us. We are in this together. And, you do still live there. I have to take this step because you've let things go. There was no food in the fridge, the house looked dirty, and it's not how our agreement went."

"I know. I've fallen down on the job. It's just that I'm busy, too."

"I know," Annie said, softening her stance. "We'll get through this together. I just wanted you to know what's up. Once I have all the details, I'll fill you in. By the way, how's the job going? Jack said tourism is about to knock on your door and make you a very busy woman."

"Oh, girl, you can say that again. But Diane and I are kicking butt and taking names later."

"How's Danny?"

"He's good. We're going to the RiverDogs game tonight."

Annie stared off into space. The timing couldn't have been better in regards to her making this stopover to the Visiting Friends Network. "Okay, you have fun. I'll talk to you later."

"Oh, hey, by the way, Diane and Richard want us to come over for dinner one night. Are you and Jack free?"

"Jack has been falling into bed exhausted. The house

is coming along, and he's now going to add another bedroom to the house plans and build a cottage."

"A cottage?" Mary asked.

"Yeah, listen, I've got to go. We'll talk soon. I'll have Jack call his sister and work out the details concerning dinner."

Annie stepped back inside the small office. The lady, still sitting behind her desk, smiled when Annie dropped down into the same chair she'd been sitting in earlier.

"I have a couple of choices. In fact, it might be nice to rotate them and see who gets along better with your family and vice versa."

"I love that idea. Tell me who." Annie scooted her chair closer to the desk and listened as the woman told her the names of the individuals and all their qualifications.

"Well, what do you think?" the woman asked.

"I'm not sure. I know the two women sound delightful, and the fact that one loves to play bridge and the other loves performances will be right up their alley. But, I'm not sure about Charles. Having a man around them might not be a great idea."

The woman tilted her head. "Why would they be opposed to a man? You said they were ambulatory, and could take care of all their hygiene, so this is purely for companionship, and to help them around the house.

Having a man could be a great thing if they needed help with a simple repair. Charles has been in our system for quite some time, and the ladies do love him. He's got a great reputation, and he does it because he's very social."

"True. I guess we could give it a try. If it doesn't work out, then we just take him off the list."

"He likes to go to plays, too, and it says here he's a scotch and cigar aficionado."

Annie's eyes widened. "Let's hope those two don't take up cigars!"

CHAPTER 11

"*I*'m going to have to use toothpicks to hold up my droopy eyelids," Jack said as he drove to Diane and Richard's place.

"I know, baby, I'm sorry. It's a very tiring time for the both of us."

"I'm sorry I haven't been around much. How's the bakery coming along?"

"Fantastic. The kitchen is done, and the furniture will be delivered next week. Re-grand opening is scheduled for the Fourth of July weekend. I'm so excited," Annie said in a bubbly tone.

Jack pulled up to the curb by Diane and Richard's house. "Here we are. I see Danny is here already," he said, motioning toward the red Mustang.

"Mary is happy with Danny, so that's a good thing, I guess," Annie said as she rapped on the front door.

"Little Brother! It's so nice to see you. It's been a while," Diane said, opening the door wide.

"I've been super busy. The house is about eighty percent completed and I'm trying hard to keep those guys on schedule."

"And killing himself while he does it," Annie said, bumping shoulders with Jack.

"Dad says you're still working full-time for the company," Diane said as she handed Jack an amber colored liquor. "I figured you could use that to loosen up a bit," she teased.

Jack sniffed the drink. "Oh, the hard stuff, huh? I guess you'll be driving us home." He looked at Annie and smiled.

"Jack and Annie," Richard called out from behind Diane, with their daughter Crystal hugging his leg.

"You see Richard more often than you see me," Diane pouted.

"I know, Sis, I'm sorry. Soon things will be more normal."

The three laughed. "Normal? The Powells are never normal," Diane said, taking Annie by the hand and leading her toward the back of the house. "Mary and Danny are snuggling back here," she whispered.

Annie stopped as she passed by little Crystal. "Hello," she said, getting down to her eye level.

Crystal rocked back and forth and smiled.

"What's the matter, Crystal? Can't you talk?" Jack scooped her up into his arms and twirled her around, causing her to giggle.

"Uncle Jack," she sang.

Jack put her up on the counter and began to tickle her. Annie watched as Jack interacted with his niece. His parental charisma was warming her through and through.

"Where did you say Mary was?" Annie asked as her eyes traveled to Diane.

Diane pointed to the back room. Annie lurked around the corner, not sure what she'd see. Mary and Danny were indeed cuddled on the sofa. Mary had her leg tossed over his, and she'd just kissed him when they entered the room.

"*Ahem*," Diane said, clearing her throat.

"Hey, Annie," Mary said, pulling her leg off of Danny and standing.

Annie crossed the room and gave Mary a hug. "It's been a while since we've seen each other, too," Annie said, looking over her shoulder at Diane.

"Dinner will be ready in about ten minutes. We have to get things cracking here before we lose old Jack. He's working on just a few hours of sleep." Diane quickly left the room.

"Danny," Annie said, tipping her head.

"What's up, Annie?"

"Glad to see you and Mary so happy."

"Annie," Mary said, blushing.

"Mary's been slamming busy at the office with Diane. What are you doing to keep busy?"

"Annie McPherson!" Mary said.

"You mean Annie Powell," Annie said smugly.

"Powell. Please don't come here and think you can push your big sister attitude toward Danny. That's not going to work." Mary put her hands on her hips.

"That's okay, Mary. I got this. Let's see. This morning I spent two hours at the VA waiting for my appointment with the shrink. After that, I went to work for the family's business, where I washed a few cars, picked up a few clients, and then came to dinner with your sister. Is that fulfilling enough for you?"

Annie stepped back, clearly not ready for Danny's reprimand. "I'm sorry, Danny. That wasn't nice of me. I'm not thinking rationally. I'm exhausted, too. The bakery is taking a lot of time, and well, what I just said was not called for in the least. Please accept my apology."

"Apology accepted."

"Kids, dinner is served," Diane called out.

Annie kept her mouth shut except to shovel in the delicious food. Diane was a great cook, and it showed with her exemplary recipe of baked chicken enchilada and Spanish rice. Jack remained fairly quiet, too, and Annie could see he struggled to keep awake.

After the heavy carb dinner, Jack really had difficulty staying awake—that and the scotch Diane served him earlier. Annie pushed her plate aside. "Great dinner, Diane, thanks so much for inviting us tonight. I promise the next time we get together; Jack and I won't have one foot in bed." Annie glanced over at Jack

"No room for dessert?" Diane asked as she slid back her chair and began to gather the plates.

"Can we take it to go?" Jack asked, helping to clear the table, too.

"Leave the dishes, Jack. I have it. You guys head home and get some rest. I can't help in the least with building a house, but is there anything we can do to help with the bakery, Annie?"

Annie drew in a deep breath. "Well, since you asked, yes, there is." Annie scanned the room, her eyes focusing on Mary. Not once had she really asked to help, except to go shopping with her. "I could use a few hands to help me decorate. The furniture comes next week. I have shelves and pictures to hang, and furniture to place. Not to mention bake a zillion cupcakes and cookies."

"I thought Betsy was helping?" Mary said.

"Betsy is helping. She's baking a lot of the cupcakes and cookies. But we are expecting a large crowd. I have Morgan helping, too."

"I'll stop over and help. Text me when the furniture comes. I'm pretty handy with a hammer and nails," Danny offered.

Annie pulled in her bottom lip. "Thank you, Danny. I appreciate that." She felt bad for spouting off earlier to him.

The four of them walked Jack and Annie to their car. Annie let the window down and put her hand out. "Thanks for the lovely dinner."

Diane laced her fingertips with Annie's. "Anytime, we love you guys."

"Are you sure you're okay to drive?" Annie asked as they pulled away from the curb and headed home.

CHAPTER 12

*I*t happened suddenly. One minute they were chatting about dinner and the next, the car was going off the side of the road. Annie blinked her eyes a few times, trying to adjust to the stark room and bright lights. She rolled her head to one side then the other. Hospital. Jack.

A nurse came in to take her vitals.

"Where's my husband? Is Jack all right?"

"He's in the next room. The doctor is with him now."

"But is he all right?" Annie's voice grew louder.

"Ma'am, I need for you to stay calm and stop moving around. You're getting all agitated."

"Of course, I'm getting agitated. I want to know if my husband is okay and you're not being very helpful."

The nurse withdrew from the side of the bed and began to look at the monitor at the IV station.

"Please," Annie said, sobbing. "I just want to know if Jack is all right."

"Annie," a familiar voice said.

Annie rolled her head and stared ahead. "Michael! Please tell me Jack is all right."

Dr. Michael Carlisle, Annie's old flame and friend, now dating her employee, Rebecca, walked over to her bedside and took her hand in his. "Jack is okay. He has a concussion. You all hit a tree."

Tears rolled down her face as she recalled the accident. "He was tired. He's been working a lot of hours on the house, and we'd just had dinner at Diane's …"

"It's all right, Annie. Don't talk now," Michael said. "Get some rest. Mary and the others are out in the waiting room. Just as a precaution, I'm going to keep you overnight. You came out of the accident unscathed. You're very lucky."

"But Jack?"

"We're running a few more tests on him. He's going to stay the night, too."

Annie drifted off to sleep after the nurse gave her something. She'd been moved to a regular room, and when she woke, Mary, Grandmother, and Auntie were by her side.

"Dear, you gave us a terrible scare," Grandmother said.

Auntie grunted as she rose from the chair and leaned over and kissed Annie on the forehead. "We love you, honey," she said, taking a step back and dropping back down to her chair.

"Jack, how's Jack," Annie asked.

"We don't know anything just yet. He has a concussion, Michael said, and he's still unconscious. They took him for an MRI just a bit ago," Mary said softly.

Annie winced as she tried to get comfortable. "This is terrible. I should have driven home tonight. It's my fault."

"It's not anyone's fault. A deer ran out in front of you. It wouldn't have mattered who'd been driving," Grandmother said.

Annie raised her head, drawing in her bottom lip. "A deer ran in front of us? He didn't fall asleep at the wheel?"

"Absolutely not. He steered right into that big buck, but it flew up into the windshield, causing him to run off the road. It was a very unfortunate accident," Auntie Patty said.

"One of the deer's legs came through the windshield and hit Jack in the head. He has a pretty bad gash on the forehead," Mary said.

"Jack's strong. He'll get through this, I know it. He has to finish Sweet Magnolia and the kids' bedrooms."

Mary took Annie's hands in hers. "Honey, I have some more bad news for you. You lost the baby."

Tears flooded Annie's eyes and ran down her cheeks. She hadn't even had the chance to verify if she was indeed pregnant.

"I didn't know for sure. I wanted to wait until I could confirm it before telling Jack."

"It's okay, sweetie. You'll have lots of opportunities to try for more babies." Mary squeezed Annie's hands.

ANNIE'S NURSE wheeled her into Jack's room. She gasped when she first saw him. She held his hand and talked softly to him, even though he never answered. She repeated the visits, sometimes three times in one day. Finally, on one of them, he opened his eyes and squeezed her hand.

"Jack, baby, you're back." She raised his hand to her lips and kissed each finger.

"I have a terrible headache."

"Let me call the nurse. They can give you something for that."

Jack shook his head. "No, I just want to hold your hand."

"I love you, Jack. You worried me to death."

"I'm sorry. I tried to stay on the road, but that buck was huge. It didn't go down without a fight."

"I didn't even know it was a deer. They told me about it. Did you know it kicked you in the head?"

Jack's hand flew to his bandaged forehead.

"But, thank God, you're going to be okay. Michael said just a few more days then you'll be coming home."

"The house, how are we going to finish the house?"

"Don't you worry about the house, Jack, we'll get it finished."

"The bakery?"

"It's going to open as scheduled. I'm going home today. I want you to hurry up and heal. Don't worry about anything else."

Jack grimaced as the pain rippled through him.

"I love you, Jack. I don't know what I would have done if you'd left me. I can't fathom my life without you."

"I'm not going anywhere. Remember, we have lots of babies to make." A small smile crossed his mouth.

Annie lowered her gaze, and a tear rolled down her cheek. When she raised her eyes, Jack's forlorn look made her shudder. Their connection was so deep that he felt her loss unknowingly. Annie held his hand and squeezed it gently. "I didn't know for sure, which is why I didn't share the news," Annie said, wiping the tear that rolled down Jack's face.

She buried her face into his chest, and together, they wept for their baby they'd never know.

CHAPTER 13

"*A*nnie, dear, where do want this put?" Diane said, pointing to the coatrack the delivery person had brought it.

"I think over in that corner. I have the umbrella container somewhere," she said, looking around at all the stuff. "Here it is," she said, running toward the marble piece. She leaned over and wrapped her hands around the heavy piece. She'd only lifted it off the ground an inch or so before realizing it was too heavy. "I need a man over here, please," she called out.

Danny rushed over to her side. "Let me get that, Annie." He lifted the piece as if it were a four-pound parcel and not the forty-pound marble umbrella stand that it was.

"Over there by Diane, please." She motioned to the

wood and metal coatrack stand that stood near the doorway.

"That looks lovely," Annie said, a warm smile crossing her face.

"What about these pictures. Where do you want them hung?" Danny held one by both corners, admiring the piece.

"So first we want to hang the wood shelves. These pictures will be mounted on the shelves between the brackets, like this." Annie held up a shelf on the wall with one hand and tried to hold up a picture under it to show Danny. Realizing she was losing her grip, she quickly put the picture down and steadied the shelf. "Well, you get the idea, right?" She laughed.

Danny took the ladder from the far corner and set it up along the wall where Annie had said she wanted the shelves, and began to work.

"I'm so happy we have the extra space now. Once Danny finishes hanging the shelves and pictures, we can start placing the tables and chairs. No need to have more stuff getting in his way," Annie said to Mary.

"How's Jack doing?" Mary asked.

"He's doing much better. He's home and resting, but he's itching to start back on that darn house. I'm trying to hold him back for as long as I can."

"You know you can't stop him. He wants to finish the house so you can start your family," Mary said, smiling.

Annie's smile quickly faded.

"Annie, I'm sorry. I didn't mean to stir up any bad feelings about the baby."

Annie lowered her eyes to the floor. "I just love this bamboo wood, don't you?"

Mary took a few steps toward her sister and pulled her in for a hug. "Do you want to talk about it?"

Annie shook her head and quickly wiped the tear that tried to roll down her face. "I'm okay. It's just I came so close to losing Jack. I don't know what I would have done."

Mary held Annie back with her hands firmly on her arms. "But you didn't. You didn't lose Jack. He's still the same ole lovable man that you married. My brother-in-law is the greatest, even when I'm a bit miffed with him."

Annie pulled her head back and focused on Mary's eyes. "When have you ever been miffed at Jack?"

"Never mind, I had it coming anyway. He's a keeper, Annie. He loves you and would do anything for you."

"How does this look, ladies?" Danny called from the other side of the bakery.

"Looks great, now you just have three more to hang." Both ladies laughed.

"Let's open these boxes. The chairs for these tables

are stacked inside." Annie rushed to the tall cardboard boxes and began ripping through the sealed flaps with her cutting tool. "Help me," she said, reaching inside.

Mary pulled the box out from the bottom and lifted it slightly, allowing Annie better access to its contents. She reached in and pulled out the stacked chairs. The girls opened all four of the boxes and spaced the chairs along the wall.

"So you'll have four round tables with four chairs at each table, and then the bar will have how many barstools?" Mary asked.

"I bought eight. I think eight will look great along the windows. Jack would be here to help Danny install it, but …"

"It's okay, Richard is coming over. He should be here any minute."

Annie glanced down at her watch. "I'm going to go home and check on Jack. I'll be back in about an hour."

"Take your time. We've got this."

"EVERYTHING IS COMING TOGETHER," Annie said as she microwaved Jack's soup.

"I wish I could be there to help," he said.

"Soon, baby. Michael said for you to be on complete

bed rest for at least one week and we've managed to not follow his directives already," Annie said, putting her hands on her hips.

"Only by two days. I got so tired of lying in that bed."

The microwave beeped, letting Annie know the soup was done. "Lunch is ready."

They sat at the table, slurping their soup, and in between spoonfuls of creamy tomato with basil, Annie drew a visual picture for Jack of how the bakery was shaping up.

"And for certain Richard is going to help Danny with that massive wooden plank you call a bar," Jack said, narrowing his eyes.

"Yes, in fact, they are probably installing it now," Annie said, hoping she was right.

"What's left to do?" Jack drew the glass of water to his mouth and took a drink.

"Just put the tables up, hang the lace toppers on the windows … and fix the outside. Mary and I found the cutest benches with embroidered pillows."

"Pillows! Won't they get all messed up being outside?"

"We sprayed them with Scotchgard, but we'll bring them in every night. What's wrong, Jack? You've been fairly quiet today."

"I just feel terrible that we are so behind on

finishing the house. I really wanted us to be in it by Labor Day weekend. I had this big idea that we'd throw our first big barbecue and invite all our family and friends and the construction crew who made it possible. Now that's just a pipe dream." He lowered his gaze from hers.

"Jack Powell! I'm surprised at you. You are a fighter; you don't ever give up on anything. I know you better than that! So it will be delayed a bit, we can still have the barbecue up there. The house just won't be finished," Annie said as she picked up their empty bowls and headed to the sink.

As she washed out the bowls, she made a conscious decision to drive up to Sweet Magnolia and check on the progress herself. Maybe once she reported back to Jack how things really were, he'd feel more at ease and not beat himself up over some arbitrary deadline he'd imposed on himself.

Annie crossed over to Buffy's leash and retrieved it. "Want to go for a walk, girl?" Buffy trotted over, wagging her tail a mile a minute and twirling around, excited for the opportunity. Annie laughed as she attached the leash. "I'll be back in few," she called out as she and Buffy exited the apartment.

After a nice walk, Annie found an empty bench and sat down. Buffy found a spot in the sun and relaxed as she watched the birds in the distance fight over a bread cube.

Annie's gaze drifted out to the blue water in front of her. Images of the wedding, honeymoon, fire, and car accident flooded her mind. She shook her head. She did her best to hold things together, but the truth of the matter was, she was falling apart inside. The stress of all that they'd been through was about to come crashing in on her. She began to tremble. *How much can one person handle?*

CHAPTER 14

"Tomorrow is the big day," Annie announced.

"I know, I'm so happy for you, too," Jack said, pulling her close. "I love you." He kissed her lightly on the mouth.

"I love you, too. You know what else today is?" Annie said as she fingered his shirt teasingly.

Jack shook his head.

"You get to leave the apartment! In fact, let's drive over to the bakery now so you can see it before the re-grand opening." Annie grabbed Buffy's leash. "You too, girl, you have to see what I've done in your honor."

JACK'S EYES grew big when he took in the bakery. "Wow, this is fantastic." He ran his hand along the table then his eyes journeyed to the bar. "That looks great there," he said, motioning toward the windows.

"I know, it really does." Annie smiled as she took in everything. "From the lace toppers to the wooden shelves, everything says sweet, homey, and Charleston."

"And take a look at the bakery goods," Jack said, crossing over to the huge display case.

"Betsy, Morgan, Rebecca, and even Peter have been helping."

Jack walked over to the side door and peered out. Annie rushed toward him and opened the door. "I love the outdoor space."

She stepped outside. Four wrought iron tables and chairs sat outside and two huge water bowls for dogs. Buffy trailed over to one and began to lap up the water. "She's right at home," Jack said.

"I think we're ready for tomorrow," Annie said, pulling out one of the chairs. "Have a seat." Jack sat down, and Annie sat across from him. "I drove out to Sweet Magnolia earlier today."

Jack's mouth fell agape. "Why would you do that without me?"

"I wanted to see the progress for myself. You'd really be impressed with what has happened out there."

Jack ran his hand through his hair and narrowed his eyes at Annie. "Oh?"

"Yes, the foreman told me they were putting on trim pieces, and by next week, after the holiday, they'd start on the tile work and floors, then the cabinets in the kitchen and a few other things. They're on track, Jack," she said, raising her brows.

"So we can go ahead with the landscaping as scheduled?" Jack said.

"I think so. It might get pushed out a week or two, but he felt for certain we'd be in the house no later than October first."

Jack sighed.

"I know. You wanted it to be Labor Day. And it still might be. But we have an alternative date if that doesn't work, and it's not the end of the world."

"It sure feels like it," Jack said, tapping his fingers on the wrought iron tabletop.

Annie grabbed his fingers and held them from moving. "No. No, it's not. What would have been the end of the world is if I'd lost you. Then none of this would have mattered. We have each other, and I have to tell you, Jack, it's hard sometimes to just not stand in the middle of the road and scream at the top of my lungs. I could totally have a pity party. I've been through so much from the death of my mother, and then my father, not to mention the stress of trying to keep Mary, Grandmother, and Auntie all happy, and let's not forget Sweet Indulgence. That's more than a full-time job right there …" she said trailing off.

Jack turned his hand up and placed it on top of hers. "I know. It has been a lot. That's why I feel so inadequate not being there for you. I want to help you shoulder some of this stress. We're a team, but lately, I feel you're the team all by yourself." He picked up her hand and kissed it.

Annie tilted her head as her eyes focused on the top of his head while he kissed her hand. "I love you, Jack."

"I love you, too. And tomorrow is going to be the next great thing to happen to you."

"No, the next great thing to happen to us!" Annie said.

"To us." Jack slid his chair out and crossed over to Annie, reaching his hand out to her. "Let's go home. Tomorrow is a big day."

THE RE-GRAND OPENING took off like a rocket. The door swung both ways all day long. People, old and young, and dogs, big and small, came to experience the sugary delights displayed.

"How are Grandmother and Auntie holding up?" Annie asked Mary.

"They're doing okay. I think I'll run them home soon."

"Can you believe the number of people today?" Annie said.

"I'm just glad Diane gave me the day off to help."

Annie put her arm around Mary. "Yes, please thank her for me."

"Boy, that Betsy can run circles around me. How old did you say she is?" Mary teased.

"Well, we can't really ask their age. It would be considered discriminatory, but she told me she's over sixty."

"She needs a honey," Mary said with a laugh.

"I think she has one. She's just keeping it on the down low."

"I'm needed over there," Mary said, rushing to help make lattes.

WHEN THE LAST cupcake was sold, Annie and Jack turned off the lights and locked the door. As they stepped back to admire her quaint bakery, Annie's eyes journeyed to the sign prominently displayed above the door. *Sweet Indulgence Bakery & Café.*

Jack slid his hand into hers and squeezed it. "Looks really good, Annie."

She turned to him and reached for his other hand. "Looks great." Then a moment so magical happened as they both leaned at the same time for a kiss. She stepped in toward him, and he wrapped his arms around her, pulling her even closer. She could feel the warmth escape his lips before she'd even touched them. She closed her eyes and drew in his aftershave. Running her hand down his cheek, she slid her hands around his neck and clasped her hands. Leaning in, she brushed her lips over his, enjoying the smoothness.

He pulled back and gazed into her eyes. "Now, that's the most special ending to the most wonderful re-grand opening ever."

Annie laughed. "Let's go home, Mr. Powell."

CHAPTER 15

It was after a full week of the new bakery opening its doors when Annie got the call. She'd literally just propped her feet on the coffee table, waiting for her cup of tea to cool down when the phone began to dance all around on the tabletop. Jack, who was in the shower, missed the comical conversation.

"Annie McPherson!"

Annie knitted her brows together when she recognized her grandmother's voice. "Powell, it's Powell."

"*Humph.* Did you go behind our backs and sign us up for some visitations through some old people's agency?"

Annie's eyes widened. *Oops. That was this week.* She'd been so busy with the bakery she'd forgotten all about the visits. "I can explain."

"You have a lot of explaining to do, young lady."

"Who visited you today?" Annie held her breath as she waited. Hopefully, it was Edith who loved to play bridge. Or maybe it was JoAnne.

"Charles."

Annie gulped. "Charles came to visit?"

"Yes, and we told him to take his happy behind home. We don't need a handyman, and we certainly don't need a babysitter."

"Grandmother! That wasn't very nice. He's just doing what we asked him to do. I meant to tell you that we'd set something up. I've been so busy. I wanted to discuss with you also about having some meals delivered. I understand they are quite tasty …" she said, trailing off.

"Delivered dinners? Handymen? What will you think of next?"

"Okay, I'll stop by tomorrow, and we can discuss this in more detail. If anyone comes to visit before I get there, please be nice to them."

"What would you have us do? Invite them in for some tea and cookies?" Grandmother said in a snarky tone.

"That would be nice. And it wouldn't kill you. See you tomorrow." Annie tossed the phone on the cushion next to her and reached for her cup of tea. When she pulled back, she got a glimpse of Jack standing in the doorway with a towel wrapped around him.

"What was that all about?" he asked.

"Grandmother isn't too happy with me at the moment. I failed to mention to her about the setup with Visiting Friends Network. She tossed poor old Charles out on his ear, or rather his rear."

Jack reared his head back and laughed. "Your grandmother," he said shaking his head, "she's too much."

"You can say that again." Annie patted the seat cushion. "Come join me."

"In a minute, let me get dressed."

"Oh, hey, what's your hurry," she said with a sparkle in her eyes.

Jack tightened the towel around his waist and proceeded to move toward the couch. "Remember, you've had an especially tiring day today. You need your rest." He dropped a kiss on her forehead as he sat down.

She pulled him close and took a whiff of his neck. "Ooh, you smell so good I could eat you." She nibbled on his neck, causing him to throw his arms around her.

"Okay, Mrs. Powell, be careful what you ask for."

Annie giggled. "I just want to snuggle. You smell so good, seriously. I smell like sugar and flour probably." She wrinkled up her nose.

He reached up and dusted off her nose with his finger and showed the powdery white stuff to her. "And you keep bringing your work home with you, too." He leaned in and kissed her mouth.

"Well, at least I bring home sugar. You bring home dirt, grime, and sweat."

"That's why I took a shower, babycakes. So you could just smell the sweet stuff." He wrapped his arms around her shoulder.

"How're things going at Sweet Magnolia? It's your first couple of days back on the job site."

"Going good. I'm really just acting in more of a supervisory capacity."

"Good, because how many supervisors do we really need out there?" She laughed when she thought of the foreman she'd spoken too.

"Paul is good people, Annie. He listens to me, even though he's in charge."

"Paul is a saint, that's what he is. Two men as supervisors are like two women in the kitchen." Annie shook her head.

"Well, how do you and Betsy work so well together?"

"Probably because of our ages. She's more like a mother to me. We have a great mutual understanding."

Jack patted her knee. "Well, going to go get dressed now." He stood and crossed toward the bedroom. He casually looked over his shoulder. "Could use some help with my shirt. I'm still a bit sore," he said, milking it.

Annie jumped up. "Well, we can't have that." She rushed toward him, wrapping her arms around him. She dipped her fingers just inside the top of the towel and felt his warm flesh. A deep tingling feeling floated down her spine, and her stomach tightened. "Have I told you lately how much I love you?"

"Every day," he said, kicking the door shut with his foot.

CHAPTER 16

*A*nnie balanced on one foot as she tried to put her other shoe on while holding the phone to her ear. "Yes, I realize she wasn't very nice to Charles. I'm on my way over there today to smooth things over. Please let Charles know I'm very sorry." Annie tossed the phone on the bed and finished getting dressed.

"The woman from the agency?" Jack asked.

"Yep, she said Charles was very offended by his treatment. I'm going to stop over there before I head to the bakery. I need to get the schedule up, so people know when they're working, too." She brushed her long hair and tied it back with a rubber band.

"Well, take a deep breath. Count to ten before you enter their house," Jack said, dropping a quick peck on her lips.

"I love you, Jack," Annie said.

"Love you back."

ANNIE DREW in a deep breath and counted to ten before she lightly rapped on the door. She could hear Grandmother yelling to Mary to answer the door.

"Oh, hey Annie," Mary said, clearly out of breath.

"What are you doing home? Thought you'd be at work." Annie stepped inside.

"I took the morning off because I have a dental appointment."

"Well, I'm going to discuss with them about the visitations. Maybe you could stay and give me some moral support."

"I don't know, Annie. They're pretty upset right now. I should probably stay out of it."

"Listen," Annie said grabbing her arm. Mary's eyes dropped to Annie's hand, and Annie let go.

"I'm sorry, but I don't know how much support I can be, but I'll sit in for a few minutes." Mary walked fast-paced toward the center of the house and Annie trailed behind her.

"Good morning, Grandmother," Annie said as she lifted her chin in an authoritarian style.

"*Humph.*"

"Good morning, Annie," Auntie Patty said.

Annie gazed over at Mary who stood with her hands clasped in front of her. "We wanted to discuss something with you." Annie sat down on the couch and patted the seat cushion next to her. Mary sauntered over and sat down.

"It's my fault that I didn't let you know first. I've been extremely busy with the opening of the bakery and helping Jack. I do apologize for not telling you. But let's move on from that and discuss how this could be very beneficial to all of us, shall we?"

Grandmother pursed her lips tightly and lifted her chin, showing Annie she'd not be intimidated by her.

"Mary is busy working, and she's with Danny now. Jack and I are quite busy as well. Once we move out to Sweet Magnolia, it will be less frequently that I'm able to stop by and see if you need anything. The last few times I've visited here, the refrigerator was empty, the house needed a good cleaning, and you two were very chatty, like you'd not had anyone to talk with in a long time. Does any of this sound familiar?" Annie rolled her head toward Mary first then landed her attention on Grandmother and Auntie.

"As you say, Mary is busy. But she went to the grocery store last night and stocked us right up."

Annie looked over at Mary who was grinning and nodding.

"That's good. What about meal preparation, though?"

"She got us some microwavable dinners," Patty said.

Annie rocked her head back and forth. "So, you're okay with microwaved food?"

"We've lived alone for a long time, Annie," Grandmother said abruptly.

Annie realized this conversation would go absolutely nowhere if she didn't up to the ante. She'd have to dig deep to beat these two old ladies at their own game. It was also apparent that Mary would not be helping. She'd have to go it alone. Annie cleared her throat.

"Charles loves the performing arts. He loves ballet and opera. Edith loves to play bridge and was looking forward to you both joining her club. And JoAnne … she also loves a good play and was looking forward to taking you both out to one."

Grandmother exchanged looks with Patty and then focused on Annie. She raised her shoulders and then slumping slightly, eased back into the high-back chair she sat in. "That does sound rather exciting," she said quietly.

Aha. Maybe she was getting through to them. "And as far as meal delivery, this is not your typical meal service. No, it's gourmet food. A lot of young busy professionals are using this service, too. I brought a sample menu,"

Annie said, digging into her purse. "Let's see, salmon with bacon and bourbon sauce, chicken Diane, cordon bleu, pasta …"

"So these are fresh food items, not frozen?" Patty asked.

"Yep, prepared fresh and brought to your home daily."

"I do like that idea," Patty said, nodding her head and trying to get Grandmother to agree.

"Okay, we'll give the food a try," Grandmother conceded.

"What about the visitors? Will you give them a try, too?" Annie pulled her lip out and clasped her hands tightly. "Please?"

"Oh, all right, we'll do that, too. But I'm not sure about the man," Grandmother said.

"Okay, fair enough. I can let the agency know that Charles might not be a good fit and just to have Edith and JoAnne scheduled. I just thought maybe with his intense taste for scotch you two would hit it off, Auntie Patty."

Auntie Patty's eyes widened. "Well, don't be too hasty in dismissing old Charles. It could be that we do need a handyman around here," she looked over at Lilly and smiled.

"I wonder how he feels about wine?" Grandmother asked.

Annie glanced over at Mary.

"Please, wipe that grin off your face," she whispered. "Once you mentioned scotch, Auntie was sold." She playfully bumped her shoulder into Annie's.

"Sometimes you have to get down in the ditch and get dirty," Annie said.

"What are you two whispering about over there?" Grandmother asked loudly.

"Oh, nothing, Grandmother," Mary said.

"Oh, now you say something," Annie whispered as she rose from the sofa and crossed over to her grandmother. She leaned over and kissed her on the cheek. "Thank you." She moved over to the chair Auntie sat in and repeated the kiss. "Thank you, Auntie."

Mary glanced down at her watch. "I have to run, or I'll be late for my appointment." She rushed over to her grandmother and auntie and planted kisses on their foreheads. "Remember, there's lunch in the freezer." She rushed out of the room, leaving Annie behind.

"I'm off to the bakery. See you later." Annie turned and moved toward the hallway that would lead to the front door.

"Dear!" Grandmother called out.

Annie whirled around. "Yes?"

"When are we going to get another boat ride? We're anxious to see your house."

Annie took in a deep breath "I'll get with Jack, and we'll make time. It's a construction zone, though, so we need to be careful."

"Have a good day, dear. Oh, and don't forget to call Charles."

Annie smiled. "I'll make that call today."

As she made her way toward the front door, she could hear them talking, or more like whispering, so she stopped and stretched her ear to hear. A smile crossed her face when she overheard Patty say how nice it would be to have a man around. Annie stopped dead in her tracks. Then she moved a few steps forward. *Yep, whatever it takes.*

CHAPTER 17

*D*oing better than she'd ever dreamed, Sweet Indulgence continued to dominate the sugar world, figuratively speaking anyway, and became a household name in the Charleston area.

"Jack, I've been thinking."

"Oh oh, that can be dangerous," he said, winking.

"No, seriously, I've been tossing around some ideas, and I think we should keep the food truck and make our presence known on the weekend. I need someone who can regularly run the show out there, though. I have the staff stretched pretty thin already. In fact, I'll need to hire another full-time baker to help out Betsy and Morgan, and probably another cashier, or two. Rebecca is working less hours."

"Why is that?"

"Why is Rebecca working less?" Annie asked.

Jack nodded.

"She is still working for her family, and she just told me they are going to open up their own restaurant, The Black-Eyed Pea! Isn't that a cute name?"

Jack laughed. "Sounds good. It will be great, especially for her grandmother's recipes."

"I know, my mouth is already watering. Also, she and Michael have become quite the item. I think he may be backing this restaurant venture. She didn't say that in so many words, but just dropped some subtle hints."

"I think it's great they're a couple. We need more love in this world," Jack said.

"I'm so happy to hear you say that. It shouldn't matter what race you are. Love is love."

"As long as they're happy, and hopefully their families, too. Then I say don't let anyone stand in their way."

"Rebecca told me her dad was a little late in warming up to the idea, but now that he's gotten to know Michael better, he likes him. They go fishing together and everything. Rebecca said if her dad invites you to go fishing, then that means you're almost family." Annie laughed.

"Do you think they'll get married?" Jack wondered.

"I hope so. They are so great together. And can you

imagine the beautiful babies they'd make? Carmel colored skin …"

"Whoa, they are not even married yet, and you have them having babies." Jack said, patting her knee.

Annie pulled up her shoulders and giggled. "I just love happy endings."

"Speaking of happy endings, the house is almost finished. Paul wants us to take a ride out there so he can pick your brain about some finishing details. Would you be able to get away Saturday?"

"Oh, that's great. In fact, Grandmother and Auntie asked for a boat ride. They want to see how the house is coming along. We can make an afternoon of it."

"Sounds great. You set it up with them, and I'll confirm with Paul." Jack leaned over and kissed her mouth.

As he pulled back, Annie wrapped her arms around his neck and held him in place. "Not so fast, Mr. Powell." She found his mouth and kissed him. He lifted his arms and circled her waist, pulling her closer. She moaned softly as he teased her with his tongue. He knew how to push all the right buttons. They had so much chemistry, he was hard to resist. He lifted her off her chair and carried her off into the bedroom. Their honeymoon was far from being over.

"GRANDMOTHER, WHAT'S IN THIS BASKET?" Annie inquired, holding the wicker picnic basket with two hands.

"I made tuna sandwiches and potato salad. Oh, and the homemade relish that Jack loves."

"When did you have a chance to go to the store to get these items?"

"Charles took me," she said with a lyrical tone in her voice.

Still holding the basket, Annie dropped her hold a few inches. "Charles took you?"

"Yes, he's such a dear."

Annie chuckled. "I'm so happy you two are getting along so well. And Auntie? How does she like him?"

"I like him very much," Patty said, coming up behind them.

Annie twirled around with the basket in her hand. "Oh, I'm so glad. What about Edith and JoAnne?"

"We like Edith well enough, but not sure about JoAnne. We're going to give her another chance before we give her the boot," Grandmother said.

Annie crossed her arms and rocked back and forth on the balls of her feet. "Oh, I see, another chance, huh? Well, remember, play nice in the sandbox. We don't want to make enemies. If you do, in fact, wish to terminate JoAnne's services, please tell me and not her, and I will do the terminating through the agency."

"Well, of course, dear. We wouldn't think of doing anything else," Grandmother said, reaching for her scarf. "Now, be a dear and help me put my scarf on. It gets rather windy out on the water."

Annie widened her eyes. *Where is her grandmother and who is this imposter?* She put the basket down and picked up the scarf.

"NOW, GIVE ME YOUR HAND, LILLY," Jack said reaching out.

Annie placed her hands on each side of her grandmother's hips. "Watch your step," she said, guiding her toward Jack.

"There you go," Jack said, taking her hands and leading her to the upholstered bench.

"Okay, Auntie, you're next," Annie said, holding her steady as she lowered her into the boat into Jack's hands.

After the two women were seated, Jack took the basket and the other items and loaded the boat. Annie stepped inside the boat and found a place to sit. She reached over and pulled on each of their hats, making sure they were fastened securely.

"I have to take a picture of you two. You look darling in your scarves and hats." Annie clicked her phone and then viewed the picture. She made the picture bigger with her fingers and then showed them.

"That's remarkable. Phones that take pictures," Patty said.

"Where have you been? Phones have been taking pictures for years," Lilly barked.

"Now, you two, no fussing on this trip," Annie ordered.

Annie and Jack had already discussed that he would take the waves a bit easier today. Their last boat ride had ruffled a few feathers. They'd had fun, and it had been exciting, but they'd both told Annie that hitting the waves hard had bruised their butts. Annie laughed about that now.

After they tied up *Lady Powell* to the dock, Jack and Annie became the crew again to help everyone off. They slowly made their way up the small incline, taking breaks along the way. When the house came into view, everyone stopped to view the beautiful structure.

"It's so magnificent," Patty said.

"It looks like an old house, but brand-new," Lilly said, almost shouting.

"That's what we wanted. The shake siding is actually cement fiberboard, and the roof shingles are actually steel," Annie said. "Looks great, but also is functional for storms."

"I love the shutters," Lilly said.

"Blue, like the water before us," Jack said, gazing off into the distance.

"It's striking, Jack. The colors are just awesome."

"I thought the light grey with the blue shutters was a great combination," Jack said.

Annie hugged Jack's waist. "I just love how the trim looks. And the lookout window is special, too." She pulled him in close.

"That's so those kids we're going to have can look out the window and see what's up." He laughed when he visualized peering eyes and noses pressed against the glass. "Come on, there's so much more to see," Jack said, leading the way.

Just then they heard a truck drive up. "Paul's here," Annie said.

"Take your grandmother and auntie inside, and give them the fifty-cent tour. Then I'll take them to the picnic table, and you and Paul can talk business. I don't want them interjecting their ideas about our house …"

"Jack," Annie said, swatting him on the arm.

"So, that's the house, what did you think?" Annie said, leading them outside.

"I loved it. What's that little structure going to be?" Patty said, motioning toward the cement foundation and the beginnings of the framework.

"Oh, that," Annie said, stumbling for words.

Lilly and Patty tightened their mouths and focused on Annie.

"A cottage, more like a guest house," Annie said with a shaky voice.

"Oh, well, why didn't you just say that in the first place? I think that's a great idea. After all, you live out here in the boonies. It would be nice to offer a place for someone to spend the night, instead of traveling those narrow and dangerous roads home," Grandmother said.

Annie laughed. "You're too funny, Grandmother. Well, I guess that'll mean you and Auntie won't mind staying over a time or two?"

"Sounds lovely," Auntie said.

"Ladies, why don't you come with me?" Jack held out both of his arms.

Annie watched as he led them to the picnic table. She turned toward Paul. "Family, you got to love them, right?"

They both entered the house. "Chair rails in the dining room?" Paul asked.

Annie nodded. "Yes, for sure. And in the downstairs half bath, I think white beadboard would be nice," Annie added.

"Okay, I think I have all of your requirements. We'll get it done. And listen, Jack's been a trooper in all of this, especially after what he's been through. I tried to get him to back off a bit, but he wanted to be involved up until the end."

Annie shook her head. "He's a man, isn't he? You guys are so stubborn."

"We'll be finishing up the cottage but probably after you move in. The landscapers are due out here next week. I told them a hundred times to not chop any trees down. They gave me their word."

"Okay, and what about for the yard space?"

"We're going with Bermuda grass for the front and back, azaleas, hawthorns, and roses. Did you want anything else?"

"Yes, I'd love a mock orange, a butterfly bush, and some lavender."

"You got it."

"I better get out there and rescue Jack. He's a saint, but it takes being more than that sometimes when dealing with Grandmother." Annie winked.

"I'll just give my respects and be on my way."

Annie plopped down on the bench beside Jack.

"Everything go all right?" he asked.

"Better than all right." She dropped a sweet kiss on his lips.

"I'm starving, let's eat." Jack opened up the basket and began distributing sandwiches.

Annie chewed her sandwich as she gazed at the impressively built home they'd be soon sharing. The color of the front door matched the shutters, and the white trim made the grey siding pop. Then it donned on her that something was missing. "Jack."

"Yes?"

"Window boxes."

He drew his attention from his sandwich and looked at the house. "Darn!" he said slightly disgusted.

Annie turned toward him. "Why do you sound so aggravated about putting up some window boxes?"

Jack sighed. "Not aggravated about putting them up, honey. Aggravated because you read my mind. While we were waiting for you, I noticed the same thing. I was going to surprise you."

"Oh, Jack, I'm sorry I ruined your surprise."

Jack leaned in and kissed her, the kiss a little more than a quick peck.

"You kids, get a room," Lilly barked.

Annie pulled her lips in and smirked. "Grandmother! You're incorrigible."

"Me? You're the one making out with Jack," Grandmother said, hunching her shoulders up and giggling like a school-aged girl.

CHAPTER 18

*I*t was during one of her walks with Buffy that Annie truly reflected on all her blessings. They hadn't come without a lot of sacrifices, that's for sure—struggling to get her business off the ground, the fire, the car accident and losing the baby, and now, dealing with elderly family members. Not to mention, the building projects they had going.

They'd walked almost the entire length of the Battery and were on their way back toward the pier when she got a cramp in her foot. Scanning the area for an empty bench, Annie hobbled over to it and sat down. She slipped off her shoe and leaned over, rubbing the arch of her foot. She wondered if she had been drinking enough water lately. She watched as a spasm rippled through her toes. "Ouch!"

"Oh, Buffy, how in the world have we made it this far and still managed to keep our sanity?" She leaned over and patted her on the head. Annie stretched her foot and wiggled her toes. "I think I can make it the rest of the way home." She slid her shoe back on and tested her weight. "Let's head home. Jack will be waiting for us."

She almost walked right into him. "Annie!" Jack yelled.

She shook her head and raised her brows. "Jack? What are you doing here?"

"I got worried about you. You've been gone for over an hour."

Annie glanced at her watch. "I'm sorry. We walked a long way today. Poor Buffy hasn't been getting the long walks like she used to. I got a cramp in my foot, so we had to rest. I'm sorry we worried you." She laced her free arm in his.

"No worries," he said, leaning over and kissing her on the cheek.

"I'm not used to someone worrying about me," she admitted.

"Well, get used to it. I can't live without you." He drew her close.

"I love you, Jack Powell," she said, tightening her grip on his arm.

"Hey, what's for dinner?" he asked.

"That's a man for you, always thinking about his next meal. That's why you really came looking for us, isn't it?" Annie laughed out loud.

Jack pulled her closer and nuzzled his face into her hair. He drew back and smiled.

"That's okay. This time out gave me a lot of time to reflect on all of my blessings. And although we have a lot of stress right now, we must never forget the good times."

"Agreed," Jack said. "And you know what good times I'm thinking about?" Jack stopped walking.

Annie lifted her chin and gazed into his eyes. "What?"

"Our life together at Sweet Magnolia."

Annie dropped her shoulders. "Me too. By the way, how are your grandparents doing?"

"Mom said they're doing great. In fact, a family dinner is on the horizon," Jack said.

"Oh, that will be great," Annie said as they continued on their walk home.

ANNIE RUSHED into the kitchen and hung up her apron. "Okay, it's all yours, Betsy. Morgan is out front, and she'll stay with you until closing."

"Have fun. We'll be fine."

Annie breathed in deeply and let out a sigh. "Family dinners at the Powells' are always fun. It's been a while since I've seen Jack's grandparents. Grandmother and Auntie are looking forward to seeing them, too. I'm just happy they didn't ask if Charles can go with us," Annie giggled.

Betsy dropped the spoon she'd held in her hand. Annie drew her head back and widened her eyes at the sound of stainless steel hitting the marble countertop. "I have something to tell you," Betsy said.

A wave of concern flooded her just then. Annie moved toward Betsy. "Are you all right?"

"It's about Charles."

Annie furrowed her brows. "Charles? The Charles that visits Grandmother and Auntie?"

Betsy wrinkled her nose and sniffed. "Yes, the same one."

Annie pulled up a stool and sat down. "I'm all ears."

"I know Charles. In fact, we've been dating for a couple of weeks."

"How do you know him?"

"He visits my aunt."

"Ahh, so Charles gets around, does he?" Annie rested her hand on the countertop.

"He's very social. Since he retired, he found himself becoming a shut-in. He knew it wasn't healthy, so he volunteered his services with the Visiting Friends Network. It's helped his self-esteem so much. Now that we are dating, he's even happier," she said, blushing.

"I'm sure. You are a very likable woman, and very striking, too. So, what does this mean for me?" Annie wondered if perhaps she'd be quitting soon.

"Nothing, really. I'll still work here. I love to bake. I need the interaction with people, too. Charles is just another …" she trailed off, trying to find the right words.

"Another form of entertainment?" Annie suggested.

Betsy laughed loudly. "Oh, Annie!"

"I'm glad you two found each other. I think happiness doesn't have an age. I know Grandmother and Auntie will be truly disappointed if Charles stops coming over. They love him. Edith and JoAnne are okay, but Charles … he can do no wrong."

Betsy assured her he'd still be coming around. Nothing would change in their arrangement.

"Okay, I'm glad we had this little talk. I better be going, or I'll be late to dinner. I still have to swing by and get the old folks." Annie stood.

"Thanks, Annie, for understanding."

"Don't give it another thought. I want all my friends to find love and happiness." She leaned over and whispered, "Rebecca and Dr. Carlisle are the next couple to tie the knot. Mark my words."

Betsy gasped. "I knew they were dating, but marriage?"

"Well, they have to get engaged first. But I feel like it might happen soon." Annie headed toward the opening that would lead her out toward the front of the bakery. She turned slightly and looked over her shoulder. "Your secret is safe with me regarding Charles. Let me know if and when I can tell Grandmother and Auntie."

"I don't want them to feel threatened at all," Betsy said.

"Well, remember who we are dealing with. All bets are off regarding that." Annie shrugged her shoulders. "Have a great evening."

CHAPTER 19

"*I*'m so happy your folks are allowing me to bring Buffy over to the party. She gets lonely staying here all by herself. Don't you, baby girl," Annie said, rubbing under Buffy's chin. Buffy wagged her tail endlessly as Annie scratched and rubbed her fur.

"No, I should have thought about that before. She's part of our family so when we have an opportunity for her to go, I think she should." Jack leaned over and patted Buffy's head. "That macaroni and cheese smells delicious," Jack added, lifting his nose up and taking a whiff.

"I think it will go great with the barbecue ribs your dad is making."

"Ribs, beans, coleslaw, and mac and cheese—yum." Jack said

Annie glanced at the clock on the stove. "Timer says

three more minutes, but go ahead and take it out now. I'm going to run over and get Grandmother and Auntie."

"All right, we'll be ready. Just call me, and we'll come down."

ANNIE SPED over to her grandmother and auntie's house. When she let herself in, she found them sitting in the living room, dressed and waiting. "You are ready, huh?"

"We've been ready for an hour," Grandmother said, lifting her chin slightly in the air as if she was a bit perturbed.

"I told you I'd be over at this time, not an hour earlier," Annie said with her hands on her hips.

"Well, our parents always instilled in us a sense of timeliness. There is no room for tardiness. It makes one look bad," Grandmother Lilly admonished.

"Well, come on, we wouldn't want to look bad." Annie reached out her hand to help Grandmother up out of the chair. "Auntie Patty," Annie said, reaching her other hand to the opposite chair where she sat.

With the two firmly holding on, arms laced, Annie walked them to the parked car.

"Jack's grandparents are going to be there, right?" Patty asked.

"Yes, the entire Powell clan will be there. It could get a bit overwhelming. If you want to go home at any time, just tell me."

"Hogwash. We'll have a grand time," Grandmother Lilly said.

Annie giggled. She'd be happy to turn these two over to Jack's grandparents.

WHAT A SIGHT they must have been. Jack had one woman on each arm while Annie held the casserole and Buffy's leash, not to mention her purse. Jack lowered his shoulders and turned the doorknob, nudging the door open with his foot. Once inside, Annie could see the crowd gathered in various parts of the house and outside. Jack's grandparents were seated outside under the awning away from the harsh sun, engaged in conversation. Annie quickly pulled up two sturdy chairs and helped Grandmother and Auntie sit down. She acknowledged Jack's grandparents by hugging them.

"It's so nice to see you all again. It's been a while," Annie said as she stood with her arm around Jack's grandmother, Polly. "You all remember my grandmother, Lilly, and my auntie, Patty?"

The six began to chat, leaving Annie totally out of the

conversation. She slowly stepped away to find the refreshments and brought Lilly and Patty a glass of sangria. "Milly made this. It's very good," she said, handing them each a glass. "I'll be back and check on you all soon."

Annie turned to walk back inside the house to see how she could help when Buffy barked.

"What's the matter, girl?" Annie leaned over and picked up the white fur ball, snuggling her neck.

"What a cute little dog," Russell Wiggins said.

"Would you like to hold her, Grandpa Russell?" Annie offered.

"Yes, I would," he said, putting his drink down.

Annie crossed over to him and placed Buffy on his lap. She'd read a long time ago how animals brought smiles to elderly people's faces. It seemed to work, too. Russell's face lit up as soon as he began to stroke Buffy's fur.

"Now, if she gets to be too much just put her down," Annie said, moving away.

"HOW CAN I HELP?" Annie said as she entered the kitchen.

"You can help by sitting here and getting off your feet," Milly said, motioning toward a chair.

"But …"

"Everything is under control. The coleslaw is done, the beans are baked, your mac and cheese is being kept warm, and we're just waiting for Robert to tell us when the ribs are done. Where's Jack, outside with his dad?"

"Yep, he's keeping an eye on Grandmother and Auntie for me, too." Annie shook her head and snickered. "I'll apologize right up front now for anything those two say or do."

Milly took a few steps toward Annie and leaned over, patting her shoulder. "Your family is so cute. Don't you apologize for a thing, because if you do, then I'll have to do it twice the times because of my family!"

Annie laughed so hard she snorted. Jack's family made her feel so welcome. "Have Mary and Danny arrived yet?"

"Nope, but they should be here anytime. Diane and Richard are running a bit late as well, something about a water heater."

Jack stuck his head in the kitchen. "Hey, Mom, you have to come and see this."

Milly followed him, and because Annie couldn't resist her curiosity, she followed, too.

Jack lifted his chin and pointed toward the backyard. "Look at Grandpa." Buffy now sat on Grandpa Bert's lap.

"She was in Grandpa Russell's lap earlier. I guess she's making the rounds," Annie said, smiling.

"I think a pet would be a great idea for them," Jack said.

"They can barely take care of themselves. A pet would just be an added chore for them, Jack." Milly slid her hand up and down Jack's arm as they watched.

"I guess, it's just nice to see them smiling and enjoying themselves."

"Anytime they want a visit from Buffy, we can make that happen," Annie suggested.

Jack peered over his shoulder toward Annie. "True. We'll just make more of an effort. Buffy is eating it up, too." Jack laughed.

Robert, Jack's dad, popped his head inside. "Five minutes."

Milly raised her arms, and nodding, dashed toward the kitchen. "Okay, we're on it."

Just then a commotion at the front entrance had Milly and Annie walking toward the front door.

"Oh, Richard and Diane," Milly said, looking over her shoulder at Annie.

Annie gave them both a quick wave and smiled.

"Darn hot water heater has a leak. We went outside to

get the cooler for the drinks and saw water all over the garage floor," Diane said, shaking her head.

"What are you going to do?" Milly asked.

"We had to stop by the home store and buy a new one. It will be delivered tomorrow," Diane said.

"I guess you know what I'll be doing," Richard said in a snappy tone.

"Well, maybe Jack can help you," Annie said, trying to help.

"Let's just try to have a nice time together today and not worry about that old water heater, okay?" Milly said with a twinkle in her eyes.

Richard came around to Milly and hugged her. "I'm looking forward to all the good food."

"Grandma?" Crystal said, tugging at Milly's pant leg.

Milly leaned over and looked her squarely in the eyes. "Yes?"

"Daddy said a bad word."

Milly pulled up and locked eyes with Richard. The entire group broke out in laughter. Milly leaned over, and with both hands on Crystal's shoulders, smiled at the little girl. "Daddy was upset about the water heater. But guess what?"

"What?"

"Grandma Cora made banana pudding for dessert. Isn't that special?"

Crystal started jumping up and down. "Nana pudding, nana pudding," she said over and over.

The group roared with laughter again.

The afternoon sun made sitting outside a bit too warm, so they decided to eat inside. Annie set the table with plates, silverware, and napkins—lots of napkins. She'd heard from Jack that his dad's ribs were super delicious, but also super messy.

Auntie Patty asked if she could bless the food, and of course, the group urged her to. They clasped their hands and bowed their heads as she spoke words of fellowship, kindness, and blessings. Annie helped her grandmother and auntie tuck napkins into their blouses and drape some over their laps. They'd insisted on dressing up, again. With ribs and all the side dishes piled high onto plates, the extended families enjoyed a barbecue that no one would soon forget.

Pushing back their barbeque splattered plates, void of any food except rib bones which were eaten clean and remnants of slaw and other items, the group moaned and groaned about how they had eaten too much.

"I hope you saved some room for dessert. Grandma Cora made her homemade banana pudding," Milly said.

Jack groaned loudly. "I don't know, Mom," he said, rubbing his stomach.

Annie pushed back her chair and began to clear the

table of plates. "Let's work off some of this dinner. Maybe then we'll have room," she said, nudging Jack to get up and help.

Jack slid his chair out from the table and grabbed the used napkins, silverware, and anything else he could. "Mom, you relax. Annie, Mary, Danny, Diane, and I have this." He tipped his head over to Danny and locked gazes with him.

Mary had already taken the cue and headed to the kitchen, the sink already filling and full of bubbles. "Load me up," she said, holding out her hands.

The five laughed as they scraped, rinsed, and stacked the dishwasher. Once the dishes were done, just as Annie had predicted, Jack now had room for some of his grandma's banana pudding.

Annie brought out the large glass bowl of pudding layered with vanilla wafer cookies. Mary spooned out the creamy dessert, and Diane passed around the bowls.

After dessert, the older folks headed to the comfy sofa and chairs in the living room while Annie, Mary, and Diane finished putting away the leftovers and giving the kitchen a final going over.

"Dinner was absolutely delicious. I must have your mom's recipe for the pudding," Annie said, turning to Milly.

"Good luck. She swears it's some family secret. She's never even given it to me!"

Annie raised her brows almost to her hairline. "Seriously? But you are her daughter."

"It doesn't matter. She teases me she'll give it to me on her deathbed."

Annie furrowed her brows. "Well, maybe I can convince her we don't want to wait that long," Annie said with tightly pursed lips.

"I hope it's a long time, but she's getting weaker as well as Daddy."

"I think Grandmother and Auntie are slowing down a bit, too. I guess Jack told you we are using the services of Visiting Friends?"

"Yes, he did. How are they adjusting to that?"

"Now that Charles is in the picture, just fine."

Milly tilted her head. "Charles?"

"Yes, their male visiting friend. They like him the best. I just found out that Betsy, my number one baker, is dating him. That might not go over so well with them once they find out."

"How'd you discover that?"

"She told me. It's a small world after all," Annie said. "*Ahem.*"

Annie whirled around to see Grandmother Lilly

standing in the doorway. "How long have you been there?"

"Long enough to hear that Betsy is dating our Charles."

Annie looked over at Milly with widened eyes. She crossed over to her grandmother. "I was going to tell you, but I was waiting for the right time."

"No time would be right," Grandmother blurted.

"You like Betsy. Why would you care that Charles is her boyfriend?"

"I don't really care, but … let's talk about this another time. I came in to use the restroom. I guess all the gossip is happening in here." She turned about on her feet and scurried down the hall, leaving Annie holding her breath.

"Round one of inappropriate behavior from Grand-mother," she said, shrugging her shoulders.

CHAPTER 20

The ride home that night started out eerily quiet. Then, Annie opened up the can of worms she'd regret. Grandmother wasn't having any of it. Annie tried to get her to listen to reason, but it was of no use. She kept repeating how she felt betrayed.

"The last one to know about their deep, dark secret," she said, being too dramatic.

"Grandmother, please, their deep, dark secret? They just started dating a couple of weeks ago."

"Lilly, dear, don't you want Charles to be happy?" Patty interjected, trying to help Annie with her cause.

"Are you on her side?" Grandmother's eyes about bugged out of her head, causing Patty to reel her head back.

"Calm down, Lilly," Patty said with disgust in her tone.

"I just think it would have been nice if someone had told us instead of me hearing about it by poking my head in the doorway," Grandmother said, raising her voice.

Annie turned her body slightly, but the seat belt restrained her from turning all the way around. "Grandmother, let's finish this later. I have a headache."

Jack pulled up alongside the house and put the car into park. He popped open the door and jogged around to the passenger side. Annie got out slowly, her temper still hot after the argument with her grandmother. Jack leaned inside to help them out while Annie stood on the sidewalk. She offered her arm to Auntie first, mainly because she didn't have a scowl on her face.

"I hope you enjoyed yourself, Auntie Patty," Annie said, walking her to the front stoop.

"I had a great time. I love Jack's family."

"I'm sorry about not telling you about Charles. I truly just found out, and I wanted Betsy or Charles to be the one to tell you, not me." Annie lowered her gaze.

Patty pulled her close and whispered in her ear. "I think Lilly is behaving like some schoolgirl who has a crush on some dude. Don't let it ruin your night. I'll have a long talk with her later tonight—after she has a chance to cool down—and have another glass of wine."

Annie knitted her brows together. "Okay, but don't fight my battle for me. If she is still resistant to this news, just let it go. She's going to have to deal with it. There's nothing she can do about it."

Just then, Jack came up behind them with Lilly on his arm. Annie stepped forward and unlocked the door, opening it for them. She and Jack helped them inside and then bid them a good night.

"I hope you both sleep well tonight. I love you," Annie said, hugging them each before she crossed over to where Jack stood.

"Love you, too, sweet girl," Patty said, blowing her a kiss. Patty reeled her head toward Lilly and frowned. "Lilly," she urged.

Waving off her meddling sister, Lilly said, "Yes, love you too. Thanks for the lovely time."

Jack and Annie walked to their parked car, holding hands. He helped her in, then just before he closed the door, he kissed her. "She'll come around. You know Lilly. She has to be rough and tough. After she sleeps on it, she'll be calling you to apologize."

"I don't need an apology. I just want her to be happy and to be happy for Charles and Betsy, too."

"Agreed. It's not about her."

Annie chuckled. "But she always tries."

"GOOD MORNING, staff. How are things going today?" Annie said in her very bubbly voice.

"It's a little slow today. I think the summer storm is keeping folks away," Morgan said.

"It's ugly outside. The clouds are so dark and ominous looking. I think it's going to drop buckets of rain soon," Annie said, peering out the windows.

"Rebecca will be in later, but she's got something she has to do today."

Annie perked up when she heard that. "Oh? Did she say what exactly?"

"Nope, just that it was very important."

Annie walked around the counter to the kitchen. "Hey, Betsy, how are you?"

Betsy looked up quickly then turned her gaze to scooping out batter into the cupcake tins.

Annie crossed the room and stood next to her. "Are you okay?"

"I asked you not to say anything to your grandmother or auntie about Charles." She continued to scoop, plop, and scoop more batter.

Annie's eyes widened as she watched Betsy work. She had a death grip on the spoon, making the veins pop out on her wrist, not to mention the anguish in her voice.

"I know, I'm sorry, but Grandmother overheard me telling Milly."

"Charles called me and said that Lilly lambasted him when he went over yesterday."

Annie's eyes darted left and right. "Auntie must not have been successful with her talk."

"I really like Charles, and he really likes visiting them. So now we're in a quandary."

"No, we're not in any sort of quandary. I will get this sorted out. Just give me another day."

Betsy put her hands together and laced her fingers. "I just made some giant-size chocolate chip cookies." She looked up with a smile.

Annie stepped closer and put her hand on the older woman's shoulder. "I'm really sorry about this. I'll fix it, I promise. And yes, I'd like a cookie." She smiled back.

Betsy put the batter scooper down and wiped her hands on her apron. Just then they heard some laughter coming from out front. The women exchanged looks then crossed the room to see what the commotion was about. Morgan and Rebecca were hugging and crying.

"What's going on?" Annie said with a puzzled look on her face.

Rebecca held out her hand. Annie gasped as she ran for her, grabbing her and twirling her around. "Congratulations! I knew it. I just knew you two were going to tie the knot."

Rebecca stood back and wiped the tears from her face. "He asked me the other day, but we had to get the ring sized. I didn't want to say anything until I had it right here on my finger." She lovingly stared at the shiny rock.

"It's beautiful, Rebecca. Congratulations," Betsy said, admiring the ring.

"When's the date?" Annie said, getting right to the point.

"December twenty-second."

"A Christmas wedding!" Annie shrieked.

"I don't know where we're going to have it at. We only have a little over three months. It will be simple though—my family, our friends, that sort of thing."

Annie lifted her chin and lowered her lids. "What about Michael's family? I recall he had a dad that I think lived in Florida."

"He may be too ill to travel. We might visit him when we honeymoon."

"Well, it will be a great wedding and if you need any help, don't hesitate to ask."

"Well, since you asked …" Rebecca said trailing off.

Annie cocked her head. "Yes?"

"I wondered if I could ask Betsy," Rebecca said,

looking around Annie, "if she would make our cake." Rebecca batted her lashes a few times.

"I'd be honored," Betsy said without any hesitation.

"We're checking on a few places for the reception, and we'd love to get married at the church on Calhoun."

"Just let us know. We're ready to help," Annie said, leaning over and hugging Rebecca.

ANNIE HAD her hands in the dishwater, when Jack came up behind her and pulled her close. "I love you, Mrs. Powell," he said, kissing her neck.

Annie shook off the suds and turned around. "Love you more," she said, kissing his warm mouth.

"Dinner tonight was fantastic," he said for the third time.

"I know, you told me already. It's now one of your favorites." Annie giggled.

"That's great news about Rebecca and Michael, too. Another happy couple," Jack said, wrapping his arms around her waist and staring into her eyes.

"I think it's great. Do you think the world is ready for them?" Annie said, almost in a whisper.

"They better be. That right there, is an awesome couple, no matter what their race is. Sure, there are bound to be some bumps in the road for them, but once people get to know Rebecca's sweet nature and Michael's caring bedside manner, who wouldn't love them?" Jack pulled her in for another kiss.

"That's what I think. People will just have to get over their interracial marriage. I really hate that term," Annie said, shaking her head.

"Well, then don't use it. They're Rebecca and Michael—soon to be Dr. and Mrs. Carlisle. No labels, just human beings that love and honor one another."

"Love and honor one another like we do?" Annie said with a twinkle in her eyes.

"When you look at me like that, Annie, I can hardly resist you."

Annie snuggled closer and wrapped her hands around the back of his head, gazing into his eyes. "Never stop resisting me." She leaned forward and teased him with little nips and bites on his lips.

Jack stopped her. His deep and forlorn look caused stirrings deep in the pit of her stomach. He didn't speak. He didn't say a word. He just led her to their bedroom. A Cheshire grin appeared on her face. *Who was she fooling? They couldn't resist each other.*

CHAPTER 21

"*I*t will be loads of fun. You love to ride on *Lady Powell*," Annie said, gathering up sunhats, canes, and everything else they'd need for the outing.

"Charles was slated to visit today. I should call him and let him know we won't be home," Grandmother said.

"I already let the agency know there was a change in plan," Annie said.

"Come on, ladies, let's hurry it along," Jack said, trying to get them motivated to go.

Grandmother snorted, and Auntie Patty squealed. Annie laughed at the comedic routine playing before her very own eyes. Getting two old women ready for a boat ride wasn't the easiest thing to accomplish.

Weighed down with all the essentials, Annie and Jack

led Lilly and Patty to the car. Soon they were on their way to the pier where *Lady Powell* rocked gently in the waters of the harbor.

"It's a lovely day for a boat ride," Auntie Patty said, shielding her eyes from the sun.

"It's hotter than you know what!" Grandmother said loudly.

"The wind that dances off the bow of the boat will cool you down," Annie said as she and Jack helped them out of the car. Annie sighed. "Take my arm, Auntie Patty."

Jack and Annie slowly made their way down the dock like they'd done many times before. Jack would step into the boat first and then one by one, Annie would hand off the ladies to him. After they were seated, she'd jump in and switch places with Jack while he untied the boat and got her ready to go. The only difference between this day and any other would be in who else would be joining them.

"What is Jack waiting for?" Grandmother said with knitted brows.

"Um … um …" Annie said, stammering.

"Spit it out, woman. Who is he waiting for?" Grandmother said.

Just then, two bodies came into view. "Them. We are waiting for them," Annie said, motioning toward Betsy and Charles.

Grandmother's eyes widened then she mumbled under her breath. "Well, I never …" she said trailing off.

"Oh, it's Charles and Betsy," Auntie Patty said with pure elation in her voice.

Grandmother gave Patty a dirty look and then turned away, refusing to acknowledge either of the new arrivals.

"Grandmother McPherson, you should be ashamed of yourself. This is ridiculous. You better be nice to my friends," Annie said with a tone of authority in her voice.

Grandmother shrugged her shoulders.

Jack helped them onboard the boat, and soon they were off flying across the waves toward Sweet Magnolia.

It became difficult to converse on the boat with the sounds of the motor roaring in the background. Annie made small talk and Grandmother didn't utter a sound. She wished she could shake some sense into her. *How would this all pan out, she wondered?*

"Oh, Annie, this is beautiful," Betsy said as they climbed the small incline.

The six of them gazed at the beautiful house with wraparound porch, complete with flower boxes.

Jack draped his arms around Annie and held her tight. "It's done. It's officially complete. We have our home."

"Welcome home kids," Auntie Patty said.

"Thank you, Auntie Patty." Annie lifted her chin and

peered over at Grandmother. She hadn't said one word. "Grandmother, what do you think of our home?"

Grandmother grunted. "It's lovely."

"It's very grand," Charles said.

"Let's take a closer peek," Auntie said, moving toward the house.

Annie stopped dead in her tracks. "The granny unit is done, too?"

"Granny unit!" Grandmother said boldly.

"I mean the guest cottage," Annie said quickly.

"Everything is done. We can move in starting next week," Jack said, wiping the tears that had fallen down Annie's face. "Don't cry, baby. This is our dream. We are going to be so happy here."

"I know, that's why I'm crying," she said, trying to choke back the tears.

"Are we going to stand outside in this heat or is someone going to give us a tour? And I hope to high heavens you have the air conditioning on," Grandmother said, clomping up the stairs as she held on to the railing.

Annie laughed. "Yes, ma'am."

Inside the house, Annie found the temperature quite pleasing, and the big surprise that Jack left for her made her eyes fill with more tears. "Jack Powell!" she exclaimed, running up to the gorgeous rectangle dining table with benches and chairs and a matching china cabinet.

"Do you really like them?"

"Like them? I love them." She crossed over to Jack and wrapped her arms around him tightly, pulling him in for a kiss.

"I figure we can go shopping for more furniture, but I wanted something special for our first home, something made with my own two hands." He gazed at his handiwork.

"You made these?" Annie's eyes widened in disbelief.

"With Paul, Richard, and Danny's help."

Grandmother lowered herself to one of the benches. Annie took note of her labored breathing. "Are you all right?"

"Yes, just hot and sticky. I'll be okay once I sit here for a moment."

"Auntie, why don't you take a seat as well," Annie said, motioning for her to take her place next to Lilly.

Jack tapped Charles on the shoulder, and the two men left the room.

"Listen, I want to put this behind us, this thing about Charles and Betsy and the big, dark secret. There's no secret, never has been, and nothing is changing about Charles. Do you hear me, Grandmother?" Annie said, her tone flashing in authority.

"I really enjoy Charles's company just as you do. We go to the theater, have dinner out, sometimes he cooks for me, sometimes I cook for him …" Betsy said.

"I get it. You like him. You enjoy his company," Grandmother said in a condescending tone.

Annie's hands flew up in total frustration. "Grandmother, stop it! I'm serious, what is your problem?"

Grandmother stiffened her back and shrugged.

Annie's jaw dropped slightly when she saw the tears puddle on Grandmother's lower lid.

"I don't know. I guess I'm jealous," Grandmother finally admitted in a low muttering tenor.

"Jealous of whom, of what?" Betsy said, wiggling in between Lilly and Patty on the bench.

"I thought we had him all to ourselves. Now we must share him," Grandmother said, staring off into space.

Betsy took a deep breath. "Well, you know what? Instead of feeling like you have to share him, why don't you try to expand your friendship circle to include me? I hear we like some of the same things."

Grandmother twisted her head and gazed at Betsy. "You'd do that for us?"

"Of course. Your Annie is very special to me, and any family of hers is an extended family of mine." Betsy slung her arm over each of them and pulled them close.

Annie stood back and watched as the once highly

volatile situation regarding Charles and Betsy now came to a close. She'd just clasped her hands in front of her and was about to give silent praise to those who work in mysterious ways, when she glanced over to the sounds of scuffing shoes.

Jack pulled his shoulders up and widened his eyes. "Everything okay in here?"

"Yes, just perfect. Let's give them a tour of the..." Annie said, breaking her thought.

"The guest house?" Jack said teasingly.

Annie smiled. "Yes, because we know how well granny unit went over." She playfully knocked shoulders with Jack.

After they toured the cottage, the six headed back to the boat. Annie and Jack could hear laughter and plans being made by Charles, Betsy, Grandmother, and Auntie. The union brought a smile to Annie's lips.

CHAPTER 22

*F*urnishing a house of this size required planning. Annie took her time because she wanted everything just right. From the wall color to the rugs, Annie made sure every room had character. Jack learned early on that whatever Annie desired, Annie got. He'd make a few suggestions here and there, but he wasn't about to interject his ideas. Except for one room.

"What did you call this room again?" Annie said, walking the long room located over the garages.

"Frog—it's an acronym for finished room over garage."

Annie placed her hands on her hips. "This would make a great playroom for children."

Jack smiled. "How about a great playroom for adults?"

"You mean like a man cave? I thought that is what the garage was for?" Annie said.

Jack paused. "Well, now that you mention it, we do have a three-car garage. We only have two vehicles, and which people actually use the garage for parking cars? I could take one and make it my own."

Annie laughed. Jack's observation about people parking in garages was right on. People rarely used the garages for cars in South Carolina. "Well, then it's a deal. I can decorate this as a television room until the children come and then it can become a playroom slash family room area."

Jack turned his back on Annie and covered his mouth to muffle a laugh. It was no use however.

"What's so funny?"

"You fell right into my hands," he said, rubbing and wrenching his hands like an evil scientist.

Annie cocked her head a little to the right and peered at Jack through half closed lids. "You mean you tricked me?" She took a few steps toward him.

"I like to think of it as more like you discovered the error of your ways. That you came to the conclusion solely on your own." He reached his arms out to her.

She crossed her arms across her chest and pouted.

"Come here," he said, coaxing her to come into his wide-open arms. She took baby steps until finally reaching him. He closed his arms around her and held her tightly. "You're not mad at me, are you?"

She uncrossed her arms and shook her head. "How could I ever be mad at you?" She leaned in and kissed him on the tip of his nose.

"That's my girl. But I have to come clean with you."

Annie knitted her brows together. "You mean there's more?"

"I never wanted this space as mine. I've already claimed the garage. That's where I made the table and benches. I knew you wouldn't care. I just wanted to see what your idea was regarding this space. I always thought it would make a great playroom." He pulled her in and kissed her on the mouth.

Annie reared her head back and laughed. "Jack Powell, I'm going to have to keep my eyes on you! If any of our children develop a tendency toward being mischievous, you know I'll have to blame you."

Jack patted his chest with the palm of his hand. "Who me?"

Annie wrapped her hands around Jack's neck and held him in place while she gazed into his eyes. "I'm so happy right now. We're living our dream, Jack. Can you believe it?"

"I never stopped believing in us." Jack pulled her in

and found her mouth, kissing her deeply. They tumbled to the carpeted floor, and Annie, not letting up on her hold, rolled on top of Jack. She placed her hands on his chest and lifted herself away from him slightly while lovingly looking at his face. Her eyes traced every crease, every hair on his head, and then finally letting her eyes rest on his mouth. "We did name this room the *playroom,* didn't we?" she said with a twinkle in her eyes. Jack lowered his eyes to her mouth, making her stomach flutter. In one quick movement, he pulled her down and found her mouth. His kisses, sweet at first, then grew more intense.

"*Ahem,*" a voice said coming from the doorway.

Jack gently pushed Annie off of him and raised his shoulders off the floor. Annie, now on her back, rose up and held her position on her elbows. A delivery man stood in the archway. Jack immediately stood, pulling Annie up with him.

"I'm sorry, we were just …" Jack said, trailing off not finishing his sentence.

Annie blushed. "You must be delivering our new furniture." She crossed toward the man, straightening her clothes, and brushing her fingers through her hair.

The large framed man wearing a thin white tee shirt and blue jeans nodded. "Just tell us where you want things," he said, turning to walk back down the stairs.

Annie glared at Jack. "Jack Powell, we could have been thoroughly embarrassed if he'd come a few minutes later," she said through gritted teeth.

"Oh, calm down. I wasn't going to let you go too far."

Annie widened her eyes. "Me go too far? *Humph.*"

Jack patted her behind as she took the lead and descended the stairs.

She looked over her shoulder and pursed her lips tightly. Then she broke out in laughter. "Who am I kidding? I can't even stay angry at you."

Jack and Annie tried to stay out of the delivery crew's way, but still be able to direct where things should go. Jack didn't direct anything without Annie's prior approval.

"Couch goes over there and tables there," she said, pointing to various parts of the living room.

"Here comes the huge desk," Jack said, backing out of the way as two men fumbled with the large mahogany desk.

"Yes, that goes in the back room, follow me," Annie said as she led the way to her new office space.

After about an hour of deliveries, the truck pulled out of the drive and headed off the island. Jack and Annie held each other as they watched the truck leave, Annie holding up her hand and waving goodbye. They stepped back and closed the front door, turning around to admire their newly furnished house. "This new stuff is going to make our old stuff look, well, old." Annie said laughingly.

"Why don't we save it for Mary and Danny?" Jack said.

Annie furrowed her brows. "Mary and Danny?"

Jack widened his eyes. "Oops! I see you didn't know."

"No, I didn't. When is this going to happen?"

"Soon. They're looking for a place now."

"You know what that means, don't you?" Annie said with one hand on her hip and the other running through her long locks.

Jack wiped the look of surprise off by brushing his hand across his face.

Sounding fatigued, Annie replied, "Yep, we better get the granny unit furnished soon, too."

"Are you sure that they can't live alone without Mary? You said yourself she's not been providing much in the way of their care. We could beef up the visits with Charles, JoAnne, and Edith."

"You should hear yourself. I think that's the sound of sheer desperation, right there," Annie said, laughing.

"I don't know … I love your family. I really do, but I

was hoping to have some time with my beautiful wife before the in-laws moved in," he said with his head bowed down and shuffling toward her like some little kid who'd just lost his favorite toy.

Annie lifted his chin with her finger. "I just want to be prepared, that's all. I think your plan is great. We'll coordinate more visits, and now that Betsy is in the loop, maybe it will be okay."

"Now, wait a second. Betsy is working full-time baking. She can't be saddled with your grandmother and auntie, too."

"Not saddled. She said it right here," Annie said, pointing to the bench. "She said, 'open up your circle of friends to include me.' Grandmother and Patty were elated with that, too."

"Okay, but if I were you, I'd be looking for a backup baker. Otherwise, you might be back in the kitchen, Betty Crocker," Jack said, smiling.

"Well, that wouldn't be so awful. I loved that part of my life, you know. That's how it all started. Me and Morgan taking the entire cupcake world by storm."

"True, but now you're married, and going to have some babies," he said, rocking her back and forth in his arms, looking up at her with puppy dog eyes.

"Jack, stop it."

"I'm just saying, be prepared."

"Oh, let me guess, you were a Boy Scout once?"

"You betcha, and proud of it," he said, holding up two fingers.

CHAPTER 23

*M*ove in day went smoothly, especially since some of the older pieces went into the garage. Annie hadn't had an opportunity to speak with Mary yet. She had to hear it from her lips that another wedding was in the future. She breathed in and let it out slowly. She wondered how Grandmother and Auntie would take the news. As much as they liked Danny, no one really knew him that well. Jack had touched on his prior military service and the internal strife he dealt with regarding his overseas tours. Annie wondered if Mary was able to handle living with a veteran. She knew there were lots of services available, and with Charleston being very pro-military and having a large VA hospital Annie hoped he was getting the help he needed. Of course, she really wasn't sure what sort of help he required.

Annie lowered the top half of her body inside the large cardboard box and retrieved the paper wrapped china pieces that Grandmother and Auntie had given her and Jack. They'd said they wanted her to enjoy them now, while they were alive. They'd also said their house parties and large family dinners were a thing of the past and now passed the torch to Annie and Jack. Annie rather liked the idea. The housewarming get-together she planned was shaping up rather nicely.

Annie climbed the step stool and placed the items in her newly built china cabinet, designed by Jack.

"Be careful up there. I don't need any injuries," Jack said softly as he held the stool steady.

Annie looked down. "Don't be silly. This only has three steps."

"I have to go in for a full shift. Dad and Richard really need me."

"They've been so great with letting you have so much time off with the move and all."

"Not to mention for the wedding, honeymoon, oh, and let's not forget the bakery fire." Jack shook his head as he also recalled the episode that shrouded their happy life and the baby they'd lost.

"But that's all behind us. We're moved in, the house

is lovely, and we're going to throw a huge housewarming party." Annie's eyes welled with tears.

"Why are you crying, sweetheart?"

"Happy tears, Jack, just happy tears." She stepped down and wrapped her arms around his waist.

He ran his hand from the top of her head down her back. He rocked her gently back and forth. "Okay, because we've had enough sadness to last our entire lives."

Annie wished that were true. But with aging family members, she knew that sometime, no matter how far ahead, sad times lurked in the shadows. She shuddered. "Yes, let's just think happy thoughts." She pulled back and kissed him.

"ANNIE! THIS IS A SURPRISE," Diane called out, opening her arms wide.

Annie walked into the hug and squeezed her. "I know. It's been a while since I've stopped by. I was in the neighborhood."

Mary looked up when she heard Annie's voice. "Hey, Sis, what brings you here?"

"I was wondering if you were free for lunch?"

Annie's eyes darted from Mary to Diane and back to Mary.

"Sure, let me grab my purse. I was just going to eat this peanut butter sandwich but a nice lunch sounds so much better. Where shall we go?" Mary stood and shuffled some things around her desk before pulling out the bottom drawer and retrieving her purse.

"Take her to California Dreaming. They have fabulous salads," Diane said as she walked around to the other side of the counter.

"I'll have her back in an hour," Annie said, looking over her shoulder.

"Take two. You don't get to have this girl time often enough."

"Thanks, Diane!" Mary said.

"Yes, you're a dear. By the way, party at our house a week from Saturday."

"You're all moved in and ready for a crowd?"

"Yep, we're very excited, too."

"Okay, text me all the details," Diane said.

The girls chatted about the weather, the new house, and their jobs. It was just enough conversation to get them to the restaurant. Annie planned to ask her about Danny once there.

The hostess seated them by the window. It was a beautiful late September day. The heat and humidity seemed to be gone, leaving blue skies and mild temperatures. Annie lifted her shoulders and sighed then picked up the menu.

She peered over the top once then dipping her eyes back to the print. She quickly folded the menu and tossed it on the table. "Shrimp salad for me," she sang.

Mary closed hers and tossed it on top of Mary's. "I think I'll have the clam chowder and a small Caesar salad."

Annie leaned forward to say something, but just then the server appeared, ready to take their order.

"Yes, we'll have two iced teas, and I'll have a large shrimp salad, and she'll have the cup of clam chowder with a side Caesar salad."

"I'll get the drinks right out and put your order in." The young woman closed her order book, picked up the menus, and took off across the room toward the kitchen.

"What were you going to say?" Mary said.

Annie wiped her hands on the white linen napkin that draped across her lap. "So … I hear you and Danny are moving forward with plans?"

Mary rocked her head up and down. "Yes, I'm so excited. We get along so well. It's been a great match."

"Well, I'm happy for you, I really am, but marriage is a big step."

"Marriage!" Mary covered her mouth to contain her loud voice.

Annie knitted her brows together. "Yes, aren't you guys getting married?"

"Married? No way. We're just moving in together."

Annie slumped back into her chair. She rolled her head to look out the window.

"Who told you we were getting married?"

Annie thought back on her conversation with Jack. Mary was right. He never actually said the words marriage. "No one. Jack told me you were looking for a place, I guess I just assumed."

"He's been living at the garage where they keep the vehicles."

Annie raised her brows.

"In a back room. He has a nice setup actually. He's saved up enough money and so we're looking to rent something out on one of the islands."

"I see. I guess you haven't told Grandmother or Auntie about your plans?"

"No, not yet. I know it's going to go over like a lead balloon."

"You can say that again. It's not that they are against you living with him. We just don't know that much about him."

"He's quiet. What can I say?" Mary smiled at the server when she placed their lunches before them.

"Well, you're over twenty-one and are pretty self-sufficient. I guess no one can or should stand in your way," Annie said, digging into her shrimp salad. "This is so good," she said in between bites.

"My main concern is for their happiness and how well they can get along by themselves," Mary said, drawing the iced tea to her lips.

"That's my biggest concern, too. We have the cottage ready and just between you and me, that's the *granny unit*." Annie laughed.

"Who are you kidding? We all knew that from the beginning. You can call it cottage, guest house, or whatever. It's the granny unit!" Mary said with a twinkle in her eyes.

"I just don't know if they're ready for that. Heck, I don't know if Jack and I are ready for that."

"I say beef up the visiting friends and see how that goes first. No need to jump in the frying pan just yet."

"True." Annie moved some shrimp around her plate before forking a large one. "Look at the size of this shrimp."

"Well, we are on the Atlantic coast."

"Okay, so let's talk party," Annie said, changing the subject.

"Oh, one last thing, Sis."

Annie studied Mary's face as she waited.

"I'm happy you're my family. I probably don't say it often enough, but I'm very happy to have you, Grandmother, and Auntie in my life. Now I also have a brother in Jack, and a whole lot of extended family. It's really great."

Annie reached out her hand and laid it on the table. Mary placed her hand on top. "We've been through quite a bit. More than a lot of families and we're continually being tested. Just remember where you came from, who loves and supports you, and never … never, give up the faith." Annie flipped her hand over and laced her fingers with Mary's. She gently squeezed her hand before letting go and rested back in her chair. "Now, let's talk about the party."

"I think that's a great idea. Peter is a great hand at putting up lights and erecting canopies. Richard and Danny will do their part as well. The older family members can just show up to the party. No need to bring a thing," Mary said, sitting straight with her shoulders squared.

"That's what I thought. We'll rent one of those huge party-size grills and do hamburgers and hot dogs. I'll go to the wholesale warehouse and get tubs of potato salad, big bags of chips, and—"

"Don't forget to make your guacamole," Mary said, not letting Annie finish her sentence.

Annie entered all these suggestions into the color note on her smartphone. "Got it. I'll buy at least one large bag full of avocados."

"Desserts?" Mary asked.

"Watermelon and chocolate chip cookies—very simple," Annie answered.

"Drinks?"

"Homemade Sangria—I got the recipe from Milly. Plus, we'll have tubs of cold beer, soda, and bottled water."

"Music?" Mary said with a sly smile appearing across her mouth.

"Danny, of course!"

"Okay, I'll let him know."

"Sounds great, Mary. Now, you let Jack and me know if you need any help moving, just please don't do it for a few more weeks. We have to get this party over with first."

"No worries. We've been talking about it for a while, but we just really started looking this past week."

"Oh, before I forget. We have some furniture for you. Jack is storing it out in his man cave right now." Annie laughed when she recalled their little episode about play-rooms and man caves.

"Great, that will be so awesome. I think Grandmother and Auntie may give me a few things, too, but I'll wait and let them offer to me first."

"How are you going to tell them?"

"Danny and I are going over for dinner on Thursday night. We'll tell them then."

"Okay, well let me know if you need any rein-forcements."

"Charles and Betsy will be there, too."

Annie pulled her head back. "Really?"

"That's what Auntie Patty told me."

Annie strummed the tabletop with her fingers. She knew better. Grandmother and Auntie had something up their sleeve.

CHAPTER 24

*J*ack gave her the down and dirty quick version of driving the boat. She didn't have the heart to tell him but she'd driven a few in her day. She didn't let on, though. She made him feel important that way.

"Show me," he said, dangling the key with a red and white bobber attached.

"I put the key here, and I turn it like this," she said, listening to the engine sputter before catching and moving the propeller. "Then I put the shifter here," she said, lowering the gear, "and then I give it some power."

The boat took off and Jack wobbled back and forth on his feet while he steadied himself. "Whoa, speed racer, slow it down a bit," he said, holding the brim of his hat in place.

Annie gazed over at him and flashed him a wide smile. Then all eyes on the water as she bumped up the speed a tad more. The boat bounced and hit the waves hard, causing her to adjust her speed. She looked over at Jack. He held on to the canopy poles, not taking his eyes off of the water. Annie slowed the boat way down, almost to a crawl, and relaxed. "Am I making you nervous?"

Jack let go of his death grip and stepped over to the cockpit area. "A little," he said, tipping his head up and down. "A little," he said, repeating himself.

Annie laughed. "I'm not a newbie. I've driven boats before. It's been a while, but you know what they say about horses."

Jack knitted his brows together and smacked his lips. "Yeah, that's horses. Not horsepower as in this boat. It has a lot you know."

"Here, you take over, then." Annie scooted over.

"No, you wanted to drive the boat, so drive it."

Annie looked over her shoulder and then hit the throttle, sending Jack reeling. He grabbed the canopy poles once again, but not without giving her a dirty look.

After they'd been gone for about an hour, she headed the boat back toward home. She pulled it alongside their dock and idled while Jack jumped out of the boat. She tossed him the rope to tie *Lady Powell* up with, shut the engine down, and gathered her things.

They held hands as they walked up to their property and Sweet Magnolia. "You know, we should think about building a proper boat cover so we can berth the boat during the winter," Annie said, holding his hand as the climbed the last of the small incline.

"Okay, so you know boat jargon, too? Who are you and what have you done with Annie? She's about five feet three inches tall, has reddish blonde hair, and green eyes. "

Annie playfully slapped him on the shoulder. He grabbed her hands as she pulled away, pulling her toward him, his mouth quickly on hers. She kissed him back as her hands made their way down his back, resting on his back pockets. She gave him a little squeeze on his back end.

"Hey, don't do that unless you mean business," he said through kissing lips.

Annie pulled away from his kiss although she really enjoyed it. "Tomorrow is the big party. Are you excited?"

"Sure, it'll be fun. Tomorrow morning the guys will be here, bright and early to help set up."

"I'll have coffee and homemade cinnamon rolls ready for them."

"Don't feed them too well or we won't get any work out of them," Jack said teasingly.

"Jack Powell!"

"I'm going to head to the garage for a bit. I'll be in soon for dinner," he said as he veered toward the garage and she headed up the stairs to the front porch.

She whirled around when she got to the top and looked out on the horizon. A burst of orange danced in the distance as the sun set. The light wind rustled the leaves both on the trees and on the ground. Annie made eye contact with the stately magnolia tree and recalled their wedding day—how beautiful the arch decorated with flowers was and everything else that day. She sighed then her eyes grew big. An idea just popped into her head. She quickly ran down the steps to the garage. "Jack. Jack," she called with labored breath.

"What is it," he said, a look of concern written all over his face.

"I just had the most wonderful idea." She grabbed his hands and swayed them back and forth.

Jack's eyes darted to their laced hands and back to her face. "Okay, what is this wonderful idea?"

"I want to bury a time capsule—near the magnolia tree."

"Say what?"

"You know, like a buried chest. It will contain some memorabilia of us. One day, our children can uncover it and they'll have something special."

"Why not just buy one of those heavy-duty tote

containers and I'll store it right here in my man cave?" he suggested, looking high up on the pre-made shelves where all the other storage containers were kept.

"That's boring. Anyone can do that," she said disgustedly.

"What would you put in it?" he asked.

"That will be revealed on the day we do it. We'll have a little ceremony—just you and me under the magnolia tree."

"Okay," he said, stretching out the word.

"Don't answer me like you think I'm crazy, Jack. This is important. I've seen it done before. I've read about it before, too." She crossed her arms.

"I've read about people filling bottles and tossing them into the ocean, too," he said.

Clapping her hands, Annie's eyes grew wide

"Annie Powell!" Jack said his voice inching up.

"Well, that's an idea. But I don't like the idea of tossing glass bottles into our beautiful waterway. I'll buy the perfect container so that it won't rot in the ground."

"I'll make something. I have lots of pressure treated wood here. I can line the box with some sort of water-proof material and I think it will hold up okay. Let me research it."

"Oh, Jack, that would be so awesome, and even more

special. Something you make with your own hands." She hugged him tightly.

"Anything for you," he said, switching off the lights and exiting the garage holding her hand.

"Jack?"

"Yes?"

"Do you suppose you could make me a wood swing for the magnolia tree?"

"Sure, I'll start on that after I make the box … and the porch swing … and the new picnic table and …"

Annie smacked him on the shoulder. "Okay, I get it. I'll stop dreaming up projects." She leaned in and kissed him on the cheek.

CHAPTER 25

Jack and Annie sat around their beautiful table he'd built, sipping their coffee when they heard the truck drive up. Jack moved his chair back and crossed to the kitchen to rinse out his cup. The truck door slammed shut, followed by a light rap on their front door.

"Come on in, Peter," Jack yelled from the kitchen.

The door creaked as it opened and Peter popped his head in. "Good morning, Annie," he said, tipping his head.

"Good morning, Peter," Annie said, getting up from the table. "Coffee?"

"No, thank you," he said, lifting his baseball cap off and scratching his head. I believe I'm coffee'd out." He laughed.

"Let's get started then. People will be arriving in about …" Jack trailed off as he glanced up at the clock on the wall, "wow, in about four hours."

Annie set out the large platters for the burgers and hot dogs and began to slice onions, tomatoes and get the rest of the garnishes ready. She followed the instructions on the handwritten recipe card for Milly's sangria and made three large pitchers of it. Mary talked her into renting a margarita machine, so they had that as well as cold beer, soda, and water iced down in large oval metal containers that imitated horse troughs.

She changed into her jeans and long-sleeved shirt, tossed her hair in a rubber band and went outside to help the men. They'd already strung all the lights, arranged the Adirondack chairs around the fire pit, and unloaded the huge grill from the trailer that Peter towed in on the back of his truck.

"I guess you don't need my help. Looks like you've done it all," Annie said with her hands on her hips, looking around.

"We still need to set up the folding tables and chairs. Do you want to cover them with anything?" Jack moved to the stacked tables that leaned up against the house.

Annie stood with her mouth agape. "Yes, I have them in the house. I knew I was forgetting something." She ran to the steps and took two at a time, reaching the door quickly.

Jack laughed loudly as he watched. "Man, did you see how fast she took off when I said that?" He looked over at Peter.

Peter nodded. "Yes, sir." He picked up one of the tables and shuffled his feet as he carried the cumbersome item to an area by the magnolia tree. "Here?"

"I don't really know where she wants them set up. Let's wait," Jack said.

"Here, here are the coverings," Annie chanted as she came traipsing down the stairs. Stacked to her chin were several plaid plastic table cloths.

Jack quickly took them from her and crossed over to the original wooden picnic table and set them down. Annie went to work and started covering the tables as she directed Peter and Jack where to set them up. The three stood back and admired their work.

"Looks great," Annie said.

"Yep, looks very festive," Jack said, wrapping his arms around her waist and pulling her close.

"Well, I think I'll run home and jump in the shower. I'll be back by around four to help with the grilling," Peter said, reaching his hand out to Jack.

Jack cupped Peter's hand and shook it. "Thanks again, man, for helping."

The three looked up when they heard another vehicle approaching.

"It's Richard," Jack said.

Annie looked down at her watch. "He's a little late, isn't he?"

Jack looked over his shoulder to Annie as he stepped forward. "That's Richard, always late to the party."

Annie shook her head and then crossed over to the steps that would lead up to the front porch. She raised her hand and waved. "Hey, Richard," she said.

"I'm sorry I'm late. I had a flat tire out on Shepherds Lane. Then, when I got the tire changed, my check engine light came on. I drove all the way home and brought Diane's car instead. When it rains it pours," he said, chuckling.

"Well, Peter and I got everything done. Sorry you came out here for nothing," Jack said.

"There's nothing I can do to help?"

Jack turned to look up at Annie, who still hadn't moved from the front porch. She shrugged her shoulders. "Oh, I know," she called out. "We need firewood for the pit."

Jack's hand flew out in front as he pointed his finger at Annie. "Thanks, I almost forgot."

Annie went inside and she could hear Richard and Jack splitting logs and chattering while they were doing it. After about thirty minutes or so, Jack entered the house.

"Okay, now we're really ready."

"Is Richard gone?" Annie asked.

"Yep, he'll be back at around four to help with the grilling."

Annie frowned. "It's a good thing Peter's coming at four or we might not get to eat today."

Jack placed a hand on each of her arms and gently squeezed. "You're so right. Richard is a lot of fun, but he's not very reliable."

"How'd Diane end up with a guy who isn't reliable?"

"It's called love, Annie. I don't know, maybe she overlooks his one bad trait for all his good ones. He's a good guy and he's a great dad to little Crystal."

"True. It's a good thing he works for the family business, too, or he might be unemployed."

"I don't know about that, Annie. He loves to drive the cars. He's never been late picking up a customer, ever."

"Well, that's good. I like Richard, don't get me wrong, but he said he was going to help us with the decorating for the wedding, and he didn't. He said he would help us with the house and the bakery, and he didn't. Now, he said he would help us with the party, and he didn't. It's a serious pattern with him."

"With Richard, you know what you get, Annie. As

long as we always have a backup, we'll be fine." He pulled her in for a kiss.

Annie tipped her head up and down. "True. Well, the patties are made and the sangria is done. All I have to do is put the potato salad out. When Mary and the ladies get here, we can handle that."

Jack smiled. "You mean we have time to spare?" He lowered his hands from her arms and laced his fingers with hers.

"Jack Powell, it's twelve o'clock!"

"Yep, just in time for some afternoon delight." He pulled her close and nuzzled her neck, sending shivers up and down her spine. He nibbled on her ear, finally landing his mouth on hers. He kissed her deeply, holding her tight. It was no use. She couldn't resist him.

CHAPTER 26

*A*nnie's jaw dropped when Richard, Diane, and Crystal showed up before four o'clock. The men chatted until Annie elbowed Jack, letting him know to fire up the grill.

"I think it takes a while for the briquettes to burn," Annie said.

"Yes, dear," Jack responded.

"Yes, dear," Richard mimicked.

Annie shot Richard a sly look. "Whatever," she said, holding her chin up. She laced her arm with Diane's. "Come on, Diane, I know when we're not wanted." The two women laughed as they marched toward the front porch.

"Yeah, you women go do women stuff and leave us here to do—"

"Manly stuff," Diane called out over her shoulder.

Jack and Richard broke out in laughter, and the tone now set for a lively party had Annie and Diane smirking, too.

Just then, Peter arrived. Annie looked over her shoulder one last time and shouted out to the men. "Here comes more relief."

Jack waved her off. "We got it," he yelled back.

Diane and Annie made several trips from the kitchen to the food tables, lugging platters. Mary soon arrived with Danny, Grandmother, and Auntie in tow. Grandmother and Auntie found a comfortable place to sit and watched as the young people rushed around, putting the finishing touches to the barbecue.

"Are Vicky and the girls coming?" Aunt Patty asked.

"Yes, they are. It's been way too long since I've seen them. We talk on the phone every now and again, but it will be so nice to see them," Annie said, smiling.

"I don't know if those men are drinking more beer or grilling our food," Grandmother said, spouting off.

Annie laughed. "Both. They're doing both. I just hope they don't burn the burgers."

"I love the taste of charred hot dogs, though," Lilly said, nodding.

"Yep, just when they have that little outer crisp skin—

almost burnt, but not quite." Annie licked her lips in anticipation.

Annie's eyes traveled toward the east side of the house where the road led out and away through the marsh and eventually toward the main road. "The rest of the guests should be arriving soon."

"What's going on with the property over yonder?" Mary asked.

Annie furrowed her brows. "I don't know really. We heard a lot of hammering going on and see that a frame of some sort is going up. I guess we're going to have neighbors."

"That's a shame," Mary said.

"Well, not really. It gets pretty lonely our here. It might be nice to see some lights on in the distance. Right now, our closest neighbor is down the main road about a mile."

"Eventually, more and more people will start moving out of the city to rural places like this," Auntie said, her eyes moving around the group of ladies.

"More people are arriving," Mary said, craning her neck to see who it was. "Looks like it's Vicky and Scott."

"Oh, and Cassie and Jessica are right behind them," Annie said, smiling.

Jack's family arrived next and then a few more

friends, and soon the back half of their property was lined up with cars.

"We should have asked some people to carpool," Jack said, leaning in and whispering in Annie's ear.

"Some did, but you're right. We'll remember that for next time."

Annie and Jack made the rounds, greeting everyone. And although they'd asked for no gifts, the large wooden table Jack had built was now covered with gift wrapped boxes of various shapes and sizes.

Everyone loved the house and what they'd done with it, and of course, everyone wished them much love and happiness. Once all the house tours were done, Annie rang the bell that Jack hung from the magnolia tree and made an announcement. "Thank you so much for coming today. It means the world to Jack and me. Before we grab our food and eat, I'd like to say a little blessing."

Everyone clasped their hands and bowed their heads.

"Thank you for this beautiful day and the food we're about to eat. Thank you for blessing us with our loving family and friends, and this day to share our home. Amen."

Amen rolled off the tongues and then Annie rang the bell one more time. "Come and get it," she called out.

Annie could hear some of the chatter among their

friends and family. Different ones asked about the sangria recipe, and some went on and on about the house and view. All of the happiness brought a smile to her face, and when Jack sneaked up behind her and she could feel his warm breath on the back of her neck, she let out a small squeal. "Jack Powell!"

"Great party, do you come here often?" His eyes twinkled.

"Thank you, I heard that a good-looking fella would be here today. That's the only reason I'm here," she said, playing along.

"Oh? And what would this fella's name be?"

Annie leaned in and kissed him then pulled back. "I don't remember, but I think you'll do."

Jack swatted her on the rear. "Kisses like that might get you in trouble."

"I hope so," she said, winking.

The chatter began to wind down as evening came. Richard and Jack piled the wood high in the pit and lit it. Soon everyone pulled up chairs and made a large circle, watching the flames dance in the darkness. With full tummies and spirits high—either naturally or from the sangria—people's smiles, even in the dark of night, brought a sense of warmth to both Annie's and Jack's souls. It was a beautiful night shared with family and friends, and one not soon forgotten.

As Annie and Jack held each other, they watched as one by one the cars maneuvered off the island and onto the main road. When the last car left, they turned to one another.

"What an awesome night," Jack said, beaming with a wide smile.

"I know, it was absolutely spectacular. I was so happy everyone made it. And can you believe that Grandmother actually behaved tonight?"

"I know, I thought for sure she'd blow a gasket when she saw Betsy and Charles come together."

Annie laughed. "And Rebecca and Michael; they are so happy together."

Jack nodded, squeezing her closer. "Danny and Mary, too."

"Yep, I hope it wasn't too much on your grandparents. It was a long night. I think your mom looks tired, too."

"Yeah, I noticed that. I'll have a chat with Dad and make sure she's feeling well."

"I'm just so happy that we were able to share this day with everyone. First our wedding, and now our house-warming."

"You know what they say?" Jack said, turning her toward him.

Annie cocked her head.

"First comes love, then comes marriage, then comes

Annie with the baby carriage." Jack kissed her on the mouth before she could respond.

CHAPTER 27

*B*ecause the accident had pushed back the completion of Sweet Magnolia, the house-warming party got pushed back as well. Before Annie realized it, it was Jack's birthday and the end of the month. They'd just had the big party so they agreed they'd celebrate low-key, with a nice dinner, a fire in their new fireplace, and a bottle of good wine.

"Dinner was fantastic," he said.

"This is nice, huh? Just you and me and a bottle of wine," Annie said as she uncorked the bottle, sending the cork flying. They both laughed.

"Yes, it really is. I love our family and friends, but sometimes it's nice just to be with each other," Jack said.

"True. Someday, we might have Grandmother and Auntie living on the property."

Jack patted the cushion beside him. Annie lowered herself to the couch and tossed her legs over his. He picked up the remote and found the Hallmark Channel, and then with the voice command to Alexa, dimmed the lights. Snuggled on the couch, watching love stories by the roaring flames of the fire, Annie and Jack celebrated his birthday quietly and passionately as any two lovebirds could.

ANNIE CALLED a meeting at Sweet Indulgence. The holidays were upon them. She smiled as everyone gathered in the kitchen around the large marble island. "Thank you, everyone, for coming in so early. I promise not to take too much of your time. As you know, this is a busy time of the year for us. From now until a few days before Christmas, this bakery will become full of customers and some will not be so nice. We've been through it before. They'll want it yesterday and we'll do what we can to help them with what will come down to their not properly planning."

Everyone nodded.

"Betsy and I have made out the schedule. I know some of you will want time off. I just ask that you see if your co-worker can swap with you so we always have coverage. I'm going to be working full-time from now until Christmas, too."

Morgan gasped. "Annie, really?"

"Yes, really. It's necessary because … Rebecca, do you want to tell the group?"

Rebecca stiffened her shoulders and sat up straight. "Besides having a wedding during this busy time of year, we're opening the new restaurant, too."

Claps came from everywhere.

"Where and what did you name it?" Betsy inquired.

"Over off of King Street, not far from here. And, it will be called The Black-Eyed Pea. Think of southern food with a modern twist."

"We all have to step it up. Morgan and I will be working full-time and Betsy will stay with her schedule. Peter, this is where I'm going to need you to step up. Instead of just being our janitor, I'm going to need you to help Betsy. She's going to train you on making cupcakes and cookies."

Peter's jaw dropped and he sighed. "I don't know, Annie. I have no baking skills."

"It will be easy. She's going to do the mixing, and you'll be scooping the batter into the cups and also dropping the cookie dough onto the trays. Then you'll be watching them bake, etcetera. We really need you. Also, if anyone knows of anyone who is looking for some holiday money, I'm hiring one or two people for about fifteen hours a week."

Peter raised his hand. "I might know someone."

Annie tipped her head. "Okay, good. Have him or her come in while I'm here. Any questions?" Annie's eyes darted around the room.

Betsy raised her hand. "Christmas party?"

"Well, I've been looking at our schedule. We have Rebecca's wedding and reception on the twenty-second and that most likely will also be a very busy day here at the bakery. Maybe we should have it the first Saturday in December?"

"I think that sounds like a great idea," Rebecca said.

"Okay, I'll make reservations for somewhere and let you all know. I think this year it will have to be dinner. We're just too busy to close for lunch."

"So, to recap," Betsy said, locking eyes with Annie. "I'll train Peter on kitchen duties, we're looking for more help, and our Christmas party will be the first Saturday in December."

"Yep, that's it. Rebecca, do you need anything from us?" Annie said.

"Just make sure my cake is baked and iced for my big day, and you all are present. I've got everything else covered."

"We wouldn't miss it. And when is the grand opening of your restaurant?" Annie asked.

"So, that's the kicker—married on the twenty-second, Christmas on the twenty-fifth, a short honeymoon to Florida and back on January sixth for a week of working out all the kinks, before the grand opening day on the thirteenth."

Peter picked up his cell phone and studied it. He locked his gaze with Rebecca. "That's Friday the thirteenth."

"We're not superstitious," Rebecca said. "It will be our lucky day," she added, clasping her hands in front of her.

"You did it on purpose?" Peter asked.

Rebecca nodded. "When you marry a doctor, you don't believe in good luck or bad luck. It's all about timing."

Annie reached over and patted her hand. She knew exactly what she meant. Michael had seen it all—births, deaths, and everything in between.

"Okay, team Sweet," Annie said, drawing in a deep breath. "Thanks for taking your morning to come in. I believe we have a plan." She scooted her chair out and stood. Everyone pushed out their chairs and soon the only people who remained were Betsy, Peter, and herself.

"I'm going to get started on baking, come on, Peter,"

Betsy said, putting her arm around him and leading him toward the kitchen.

Annie bent down to the wooden desk and cabinet that Jack had built and turned on the sound system. Soon holiday songs piped through the wireless speakers. She began brewing coffee, and decorating the shop for the holidays while she hummed the tunes she'd grown to love this time of year.

Annie pulled out the step stool and began to hang greenery from the shelves. She placed the collection of holiday snow globes she'd purchased, arranging them just so. She hung up a wreath on the front door and draped garland across the display case, securing red velvet stockings with the names of each employee embellished in gold glitter. On the top of the display case she placed an old-time Santa Clause she'd made in ceramic class pre-Jack days. She stepped back and admired her work. She drew her hand to her chin and thumbed it a couple of times. *Something is missing.*

"Betsy, I'll be back before we open. I have to run to the store."

SHE CUT the box open and put the five-foot artificial tree together. Thankfully, it came in only a few pieces. She draped the red tree skirt around the bottom and placed the empty wrapped gift boxes around it. She stood back and admired the lit tree. "There, now it's perfect."

Betsy came out of the kitchen and peered over the counter. "Everything looks great, Annie. You're just missing one thing."

Annie whirled around and placed her hands on her hips. She thought the last missing piece was the tree. "What?"

"The reason for the season," she said, winking.

Annie stood motionless. How could she forget? "You're right, we need a nativity scene. I'll be right back." She rushed over to the chair and grabbed her purse and moved toward the front door.

"Don't forget your coat, it's chilly out," Betsy said, pointing to the dark blue peacoat hanging on the coatrack.

Annie darted back to fetch her coat. "'Thanks," she said, breathing hard. "Back in a jiffy."

"Take your time, we don't need any more accidents," she called out after Annie.

When Annie returned, she sat down for a moment to catch her breath. It wasn't like her to be so out of breath … and tired.

"Did you get it?" Betsy said, coming out of the kitchen.

Annie slouched down in the chair.

"Are you all right?" Betsy asked, coming out from behind the counter display and standing in front of Annie.

"I don't feel great. It's probably nothing, or maybe I'm coming down with the flu."

Betsy peered at her through half closed eyes. She took a few steps closer, placing her hand on Annie's forehead. "No fever," she said.

"I just feel yucky." She sat up straighter. "Anyway, I got it. What do you think?" She pointed to the nativity scene that now sat on the opposite side of the display counter with the old-time Santa Claus.

"Looks wonderful there, I love it. Why don't you go home and rest, Annie?"

"I can't, I'm holding down the fort." She glanced at her watch. "We open in an hour."

"Maybe I can call in Morgan?" Betsy said.

Annie shook her head. "We need more help. I hope Peter comes through for us."

"I can place an ad online," Betsy said.

Annie furrowed her brows. "Why didn't I think of that?"

"Because you're pregnant and you have the beginnings of pregnancy brain."

Annie widened her eyes. "Huh?"

"I think you're pregnant."

Annie slouched into the chair again. She might be.

She'd been so busy she hadn't kept track of things. Annie widened her eyes. "Jack must know, too."

"How? I mean, why?" Betsy sputtered.

"He just sang a rhyme to me the other day. He said, 'First comes love, then comes marriage, then comes Annie with the baby carriage.'"

Betsy reeled her head back and laughed so loudly that Peter came out of the kitchen. She waved him off, telling him they were fine.

"I better go to the doctor and have a test."

"Go to the drugstore and buy one of those home pregnancy tests," Betsy advised.

CHAPTER 28

"What's the special occasion?" Jack asked, motioning to the table set with Annie's grandmother's china and silverware.

Annie crossed the room and poured Jack a glass of wine. "Can't I make my honey a special dinner without him being suspicious?" Annie quickly turned her back on him, concealing her wide smile.

"Well of course, you can. But after putting in a full day's work at the bakery, I just thought—"

"Sit down," she said, not letting him finish.

"Yes, ma'am." He slid out the chair and lowered his body to the seat, scooting the chair forward slightly.

Annie rushed back into the kitchen and placed the cordon bleu on the platter and surrounded them with baked baby potatoes and carrots. She tossed the warmed corn muffins in a towel and then put them in a basket. She carried the meat platter in one hand and the muffins in the other. She set them down in front of Jack.

Jack's eyes widened and he leaned forward, taking in a long whiff of the great smelling food. "Oh, wow, cordon bleu!" He picked up the large fork and gently lifted one to his plate. He scooped some veggies and grabbed a muffin.

Annie fixed her plate. "Bon appétit," she said.

"This is delicious," he said, taking bite after bite.

"I'm glad you're enjoying it. It might be the last time I cook a large meal like this." She studied his face.

Jack put his fork down, a worried expression crossing his face. "What's wrong? Are you sick? Tell me the truth," he said, rambling on.

Annie laughed. "Well, nothing is wrong exactly, and I wouldn't say that I'm sick. Although, I'll probably be sick off and on …" She smiled, waiting for him to catch on.

Jack turned his body completely in his chair and faced her. His jaw dropped. "Are you saying what I think you're saying?"

Annie nodded.

Jack pushed back his chair and lunged toward Annie, grabbing her around the shoulders and hugging her tightly. "We're going to have a baby?"

"Yes, Jack. You're squeezing me a bit hard. I can hardly breathe," Annie said, trying to shake him lose from the death grip he had on her.

"I'm sorry, baby. I'm just so darn excited. This is great news. We're having a baby." He stood up and smiled, causing Annie to smile back. "When are you due?"

"I haven't seen a doctor yet. I took one of those home pregnancy tests. Actually," Annie said, laughing, "Betsy diagnosed me before I got the results."

"Betsy?"

"Yep, I wasn't feeling well today at the shop. She said I was pregnant."

"Well, I'll be. When do you think the baby will be born?"

"To my best calculation, I think he or she will enter our lives around the end of June."

"Can I tell anyone?" Jack blinked his eyes a couple of times.

"Let's wait until I see the doctor. I made an appointment for early next week. After he confirms it, we'll share the good news."

Jack slowly moved back to his chair and sat down. "It's hard for me to finish my dinner with this good news."

"Now, Jack. I spent a lot of time fixing this great

dinner, so let's enjoy it." Annie picked up her crystal goblet that held a clear liquid. "To our new addition," she said, raising her glass.

Jack raised his glass to hers. His eyes darted from her drink to his. "Ah ha! I should have paid more attention. I should have known you were pregnant because you're not drinking any wine with me." He clanked his glass with hers then took a sip.

"Yep, no more wine for me." She leaned in and put her elbows on the table. "We need to do the keepsake box thing."

"I have it done. When do you want to do it?"

PICKING a day to bury the time capsule box proved to be a bit of a challenge. The weatherperson had forecasted rain the entire week. With a break in the weather, the two quickly raced to the large magnolia tree, Jack, armed with a shovel and the box, and Annie with a baggie tucked away in her raincoat pocket. The two quickly got to work, Jack digging a hole that would fit the eight by eight wooden box, lined with sheet metal, and Annie holding the umbrella over them to keep the light sprinkles off.

"Okay, I think that is about right," he said, lowering the box for one last measurement check.

Annie sighed. "Okay, go ahead and lift it up and open it. I'll go first." She dug into her pocket and retrieved the sealed baggie.

Jack did as she asked.

She unfolded a very small card and showed it to Jack. "Do you remember this?"

He squinted as he read the print, nodding slowly. "Yes, it's my business card."

"Not just any business card. No, this is the one you gave me on our first meeting." Annie leaned over and dropped it into the box.

Jack drew in a deep breath and removed a white envelope. He opened the flap and retrieved a tiny ziplock bag, the kind that jewelry is sometimes in. "Do you know what this is?" He held it out for her inspection.

"Hair?"

"Not just any hair, but a lock of yours."

"When and where did you get a lock of my hair?"

"Remember the night we came back from our boat ride and it was pouring rain?"

"Yes."

"I found it in the car the next day."

Annie tipped her head back. "I remember that. I got my hair stuck in the seat belt somehow."

Jack tossed the lock of hair, bag and all, into the box.

Annie dug her hand inside her pocket and pulled out a

napkin. "From the restaurant," they both said at the same time. They both chuckled at their timing. Annie tossed the napkin in the box.

By the time they were finished, they'd tossed in restaurant menus, pictures, love notes that had been scribbled on small pieces of paper, and lastly, their wedding announcement.

"I think this is a good representation of our journey, don't you?" Annie said as she watched him lower the box into the hole.

"Yes, I do," he said, handing her the shovel.

Annie covered the box with the dirt and then Jack patted it down with his foot.

"I have one more surprise. I'll be right back." Jack ran across the front lawn toward the back of the house.

Annie furrowed her brows as she watched him run. She figured he was going to the garage, but why had her stumped. Her smile widened broadly and her eyes lit up when she noticed him carrying a swing.

"I made the swing," he said, clearly out of breath carrying the wooden seat, rope, and a ladder.

"Oh, Jack, thank you. It means that much more to me now that we're having a baby."

He leaned the ladder up against the tree. He swung the heavy-duty rope over the fattest limb and then secured the rope through the holes in the wooden seat. He then threaded a washer through the ends and tied them off with knots. He swung on it a few times, ensuring it would hold weight. He jumped off and made a sweeping motion with one arm. "Try it."

Annie jumped on the swing and pumped her legs a few times. "This is perfect."

Jack caught the swing and stopped it. He held the swing steady with his hands on the rope. "I love you, Annie."

Annie slipped off the seat and wrapped her arms around his neck. "I love you, too."

"Every time you swing on this, or every time our child does, you can also remember the day we buried the keepsake box."

"I'll always remember this day." She lifted herself on her tiptoes and kissed him.

The two held hands as they made their way to the front porch of Sweet Magnolia. But not before thunder cracked and a bolt of lightning came out of the sky, followed by buckets of rain.

"Run," Jack said, pulling Annie to safety.

The two made it and stood on the front porch and watched as the nasty storm came ashore. Annie shivered. "Coffee?" she asked, looking up at Jack with playful eyes.

"I'll start the fire," he said, leading her inside.

CHAPTER 29

"*O*ur first major holiday with the family in our new house," Annie said, climbing the short stepladder to get the giant turkey platter down.

"Be careful up there," Jack called out as he set plates around the table.

"Honey, I'm only a couple of months pregnant. The doctor says everything is great. Stop worrying."

Jack tossed her a grin and went back to setting the table. "I'm glad I made a leaf for this table."

"It will be so nice to have all of us here. Fourteen of the best people I know," Annie said, crossing over to Jack and placing her hand on his shoulder.

"I'm so happy our families get along so well. What would we do if they didn't?"

Annie shook her head. "I'm just glad that they do."

"That turkey smells great, Annie."

"Turkey, dressing, sweet potato casserole, asparagus, rolls …"

"Cranberry sauce," Jack said, nodding.

"Cranberry sauce, oh, and mashed potatoes and gravy," Annie said, delighted she named everything.

"Dessert?!"

"A hummingbird cake, thanks to Betsy," Annie said.

"What's a hummingbird cake?"

"It's a moist spice cake with pineapple and bananas—and a cream cheese frosting."

"No pie?" Jack said, pouting.

"Yes, your mom is bringing an apple and a pumpkin pie." Annie playfully smacked him on the shoulder.

EVERYONE GATHERED AROUND THE TABLE. Even with the leaf inserted, their shoulders bunched up in a few places, but Danny and Mary didn't mind sitting so close together. Annie had to remind them a few times to behave … their hands were everywhere but in their laps.

"Jack, please help me with the turkey," Annie asked.

Annie scooped out the dressing from the bird and piled it high into a bowl. Jack carved the turkey with the electric knife while Annie dished up the mashed potatoes.

She ran her hand across her forehead and wiped the beads of sweat on her apron.

"Are you okay, honey?" Jack asked as he layered the slices of turkey on the platter.

"Yes, I'm feeling a bit warm. It'll be nice to sit down." She took the first dish into the dining room and placed it on the table. Jack came up behind her and set the huge platter in the middle.

Once the table was set with all the dishes, Annie and Jack took their places at each end of the table. And like every meal, they bowed their heads and said a blessing before digging in. But this time, right after the blessing, Annie and Jack had a few more words to share.

"Before we start to eat, we have an announcement to make," Jack said, gazing at Annie from across the table.

Annie cleared her throat. "Well, since I'm starving, let's just get right to the point." She pulled in her bottom lip as her eyes darted around the table. When her eyes landed on Grandmother, Grandmother nodded slowly and a sly grin crossed her face. *She knew*! Annie swallowed down the lump that formed in her throat and moved her gaze back to Jack. "We're having a baby," she shouted.

All of a sudden, the entire room broke out in total chaos. Everyone started talking to each other and shouting out things. Annie's eyes widened as she watched her crazy family celebrate the news. After a few minutes, everyone quieted down and the only noises that could be heard were the scraping of bowls and plates and the clanking of utensils as they all enjoyed their dinner.

After dinner, no one would allow Annie to lift a finger in the kitchen. Mary, Milly, and Diane, along with Richard, Danny, and Jack cleared the table and stacked the dishwasher.

"You all go sit down in the living room," Milly said, waving her hands wildly shoeing them out.

Grandpa Russell and Grandpa Bert sat with Annie and Jack's dad, Robert. Buffy sat on Grandpa Bert's lap. She knew only too well where the handouts came from. Bert fed her bites from the table all evening, and Annie didn't have the heart to call him out on it.

"Get used to it, honey. We only have one little one. It's been a while since we had a baby in the house," Grandpa Bert said.

"Yes, let's see. Crystal and our baby will be cousins. How exciting," Annie said.

"Are you planning on working still?" Robert asked.

"Yes, I feel fine. I'm sure this pregnancy will be as normal as they come. I'm just feeling a bit fatigued right now. This was a large crowd to feed."

"We won't make you do it for Christmas," Grandpa Russell said.

"Who's ready to get beat in Monopoly?" Jack said, clearing the coffee table.

"I call the dog," Annie said.

After playing the game for about two hours, everyone gave in, and crowned Jack the winner.

"Here, take all my money," Danny said shoving the play dollars toward him.

"And all of my property," Mary said with her lower lip stuck out.

Annie shook her head back and forth fiercely. "Jack Powell does it again and the crowd cheers," she said with a snappy tone.

"I asked y'all from the very beginning, who wanted to get beat. Didn't I?" he asked, looking around the room.

Annie gawked at him. "Whatever. Who's ready for dessert?"

Grandmother Lilly, Auntie Patty, and Jack's grand-mothers, Polly and Cora, served dessert.

BY THE TIME the family left, Annie could hardly keep her eyes open. "I'm just so tired," she said, shaking her head. "I don't really understand it."

"And the doctor said everything was okay?" Jack said through peering eyes.

"Yes. They did take some bloodwork. I'll follow up on that after the weekend," Annie said, climbing into bed and pulling the covers up. "Thanks for all the help tonight," she said, leaning forward and waiting for a kiss.

Jack leaned in and met her mouth. "You're welcome. Let's just take it easy the rest of the weekend. You've been putting in a lot of hours at the bakery."

Annie rose up and scooted toward the headboard. "Tomorrow is Black Friday. I have to go in, I'm on the schedule. The girls wanted to go Christmas shopping." She reeled her head back, gently hitting the wood headboard.

"Okay, let me think about this for a second." He strummed his fingers on his chin.

Annie turned slightly and snickered. "Baby, there's nothing you can do. Betsy and I are on the schedule and that's that."

Jack grabbed his phone off the nightstand and began texting.

"Who are you texting?"

He stared at his phone then began to nod. He laid the phone back on the nightstand. "It's all taken care of. You have the day off tomorrow."

Annie lifted her brows. "Huh?"

"Peter is coming in."

"Peter?"

"Yes, Peter. And, I promised him I would stop by and see if he needed any help."

"If he could just hold the fort down for half of my shift, I'm sure I'll feel much better by noon."

"Get some sleep," Jack said, patting her hand.

SLEEPING IN, sipping hot tea, snuggled on the couch, and being served scrambled eggs and toast made Annie smile. It was just what she needed. Jack knew her so well. "Thank you, Jack. This is just what I needed. How did you know?"

"Because we have that connection," he said, taking two fingers and moving them back and forth from his eyes to hers and back to his.

Annie laughed. "Yes, we definitely have a connection," she said, snuggling in close.

He wrapped his arm around her shoulders and held her tightly. "I love you. I want you to be extremely careful the first trimester."

Annie furrowed her brows and reeled her neck back and stared. "How did you become such an expert on the first trimester?"

"I know these things," he said, rocking his head back and forth.

"Uh huh." She drew in a sip of her tea.

"Anyway, isn't that what they say?"

"Yes, Jack, that's what they say. But I don't need two doctors. Let's just do what the real doctor says. I love that you're being so attentive, I really do, but don't spoil me too much. I might get used to it." She reached up and put her hands around his neck and pulled him in for a kiss.

"I want to spoil you. And our baby."

"This child of ours will have so much love. Our families will see to it that you aren't the only one spoiling him or her."

"Annie?"

"Yes?"

"Do you think we're having a boy or a girl?"

Annie chuckled. "I haven't a clue. They'll tell us when it's time. For now, let's just hope for a happy and healthy baby."

Jack leaned over and kissed her again.

Even though the miscarriage was brought on by the accident, Annie knew Jack's overprotection was a result of that sad day. If she were to be completely honest, she thought about it as well.

CHAPTER 30

*J*ust as Annie had predicted and shared with her employees, the holiday time at the bakery, although extremely busy, brought happy moments to Sweet Indulgence as well. Children, along with their parents and grandparents, not to mention their furry friends, made selling cupcakes and cookies a pure joy.

Annie was feeling better as the days went on. She made sure she took her prenatal vitamins, got plenty of rest, and ate small but frequent meals to ensure her blood sugar stayed even. The bloodwork came back indicating that she was a bit low on iron, which explained her fatigue.

Fortunately for her, twin brothers came in to inquire about the part-time hours and Annie couldn't wait to get them on board. They were fast learners too, so before she realized, Toby and Keith, were on the schedule.

"I just have to tell you how funny it seems to have two employees with the names Toby and Keith," Annie said, giggling as she took off her apron.

The two young guys laughed. "Yeah, we hear that a lot," they said, referring to the country singer Toby Keith. My mom has an infatuation with him," Toby said wincing.

"Well, I won't forget your names, that's for sure. And with pregnancy brain looming, that's a good thing." She smiled, her eyes meeting first Toby's then Keith's. "I'm headed out for the day. Ms. Walker is here if you need anything," she said, looking at the schedule. "And Morgan will be in later."

"Have a good evening," Betsy called out.

Annie stepped back around and poked her head in the kitchen. "How's the wedding cake plan coming along?"

Betsy sighed, lifting her shoulders up and down. "Good, except she's changed the order three times."

Annie laughed. "Brides, they can be so fickle."

"It's a good thing I love that Rebecca or I'd tell her to go find another baker," Betsy said, tipping her head back and forth.

"I know, she's stressed—her wedding and a new

restaurant opening. I feel her pain." Annie turned to leave.

"Oh, Annie?"

Annie stopped and whirled around. "Yes?"

"I'm a little concerned about Lilly."

Annie tilted her head. "Why?"

"Her breathing is becoming more labored, and she's wheezing a lot more. I think she should be checked out."

Annie's eyes grew wide. Her heart dropped like an iron anchor to the pit of her stomach. She'd not been paying attention. With the bakery, holidays, and pregnancy, she'd forgotten about some of the people she loved the most. "Betsy, I'm ashamed of myself. I should have paid more attention. Of course, I'll make the appointment right away." She lowered her head.

Betsy put down her spatula and moved toward Annie. "It's not your fault. They're getting up there in age. It's probably nothing, but better to have the doctor confirm it. And, on a positive note, we're all going to the Christmas musical at the performing arts center and have dinner afterward. Does that sound like the evening for someone who is sick?"

Annie shook her head. "Grandmother won't give up until she has to."

Betsy nodded. "Can you blame her?"

As soon as Annie got in her car she called Grandmother's doctor. And while she had the appointment clerk on the phone, she made an appointment for Auntie Patty, too. No reason to take any chances.

"I DON'T KNOW why you insist on taking me to the doctor," Lilly said, clearly upset by the visit.

"I want to make sure you and Auntie are okay. It's been a while since you've been. You might need some shots or something," Annie said, quickly trying to cover the real reason for the visit.

"Shots? You say that like we're some family pet," Lilly said.

"Well, you're my family and I also love my Buffy, too." Annie giggled.

Lilly heaved her shoulders back and forth, up and down. "Well, I feel fine."

The doctor called Annie in first to ask her why the visit. She told him their observations. She waited out in the lobby while he examined her. While Auntie was examined, Lilly and Annie waited.

After the examinations, the doctor called them all in together. "First of all, I think you both are in pretty darn good shape for your age. I'm going to have you go to the lab and have some blood drawn. After we get the results,

I'll know for sure what to do. In the meantime, keep doing what you've been doing. If you feel any pain or sudden feeling like you can't breathe, call 9-1-1."

THE DAY of Rebecca and Michael's wedding proved to be challenging. It rained all day, and Betsy, alarmed about the cake becoming a ruined mess, consulted with Annie about the best way to transport the cake.

Jack came to the rescue like he did on most challenges, and backed the van up to the back door of the bakery. With Jack on one side and Annie on the other, they quickly carried the round disc with the cake on top to the van while Betsy held a clean plastic garbage bag high above it. Once it was placed safely inside, Betsy rode in the back with it, ensuring it didn't topple over.

They arrived at the restaurant, The Black-Eyed Pea, where the reception would be held. Although not yet open to the public, it was the perfect place to host their reception. Annie, Morgan, Betsy, Milly, and Diane, along with some of Rebecca's family and friends, decorated the restaurant and when they were satisfied with how it all looked, they headed to the church.

Everyone gasped and oohed and awed when she walked down the aisle, holding her dad's arm. Everything from her flaring, full, floor-length gown in white to the wreath headpiece decorated with greenery and flowers exuberated perfection and glamor. The ear-to-ear smile on Michael's face showed his excitement and his love for Rebecca.

A warm feeling traveled up Annie's back and made her face blush. She laced her arm with Jack's. "They look so lovely together."

He leaned over and whispered in her ear. "Yes, they do. I'm so happy for them."

After the ceremony everyone headed over to the restaurant. When it came time to toast the happy couple, Annie drank apple cider. She drew in a deep breath and let it out slowly. It was worth it. There'd be other moments when she could celebrate with champagne. Like after the birth of their baby.

ON CHRISTMAS MORNING, Jack and Annie sat on their couch staring at the lit tree with presents underneath it, sipping hot cocoa. After a breakfast of homemade cinnamon rolls and bacon, the two were cozy and full. Annie leaned her head on Jack's shoulder with Buffy curled up at her feet. "I'm so happy your family convinced me to let them host tonight's dinner."

"Me, too. There'll be plenty of times for more hosting here." He kissed her on the cheek. "Ready to open some presents?" He leaped off the couch and left the room. Annie watched as he ran down toward the back of the house. "I'll be right back."

Annie sipped on her hot chocolate while she waited. Soon she could hear him breathing heavily as he approached. Her eyes lit up when she saw what he carried. "A cradle!"

He set it down near her. "Yes, I made it with my own two hands."

"It's beautiful," she said, a tear rolling down her cheek.

"Aw, baby, I didn't mean to make you cry." He leaned forward and hugged her.

"I'm just a hot mess," she said, covering her face with her hands.

"You're not a hot mess. You're a beautiful woman, carrying my child."

"Well, thank you for saying that. I hope as time goes on you'll feel the same way." She gazed up at him.

"Without a doubt," he said, lowering his body next to hers on the sofa.

"I have something for you, too." She rose from the sofa and retrieved a small wrapped gift.

He smiled as he examined the box. "Wrapping paper

with little dogs on it, how cute." He tore into the package and when he lifted the brown leather piece, he just stared at it for a moment. "A collar? For Buffy?"

Annie laughed. "No, silly, for …"

Just then then they heard a light rap on the front door.

"Just in time, too," she said, getting up to answer the door.

Mary and Danny came in with a bundle in their arms and Jack's eyes about popped out of his head. "A puppy! You got me a puppy?" He leaped up from the couch and rushed over to the cream-colored fur ball. "He's beautiful," he said, taking the pup from Mary's arms.

"He's a she. I figured we might as well get that big dog you've been wanting. But don't forget about my baby Buffy," Annie said, talking baby talk as she patted Buffy's head.

"I'd never forget about her," Jack said, putting the dogs' noses together so they could sniff one another. Buffy turned her head.

Everyone started laughing.

"And that's how it happens," Jack said.

"How what happens?" Annie asked.

"When the queen bee gets her nose out of joint."

Annie laughed. "She'll get used to her."

"Well, we are off to Grandmother's, see you later, Sis," Mary called out.

"Merry Christmas, you two," Jack said.

Jack got down on the floor with the puppy. "Come here, Buffy, come on. Come say hi to Isla."

"Isla?" Annie said.

"It means island in Spanish."

Annie tilted her head. "I like it. Hey, maybe you should name the children, too."

Jack bounced the puppy on his knee while he petted Buffy. Annie leaned back with her head resting on the couch back. Happy as a clam and satisfied beyond her wildest dreams, Annie laid her hand across her tummy. A wide smile crossed her face.

*G*randmother and Auntie were doing pretty well and once their tests came back, the doctor administered some medications for Lilly's heart and Patty's high cholesterol. Annie was happy she'd listened to Betsy and taken them to the doctor. Now, they'd receive treatment, and hopefully be around for a while longer and see their new great-grandchild and great-grandniece or nephew.

With each passing month, Annie grew larger. It wasn't just her tummy that grew, but her business grew by leaps and bounds, and soon she was hiring again.

Rebecca and her family opened The Black-Eyed Pea restaurant as planned, and it became one of Jack and Annie's favorite places. The shrimp and grits were to die for.

After a short phase of Buffy ruling the roost, the two dogs got along well and Buffy and Isla could be found cuddling in front of the fireplace during cold winter nights, and romping outside on the island exploring.

And because Annie and Jack were so fondly thought of in their circle of friends and family, the hugest baby shower ever took place on the property of Sweet Magnolia. But this time, Annie didn't lift a finger. And, while having her friends and family by her side as she opened up the cutest outfits and tasted the best baby shower cake ever—thanks to Betsy—the news that her oldest friend, Vicky dropped on her was just … icing on the cake!

"I know this is your special day, Annie, and I wouldn't dream of stealing your thunder, but I have some great news myself." Vicky beamed as she waited for Annie's response.

"Are you expecting, too?"

"No, but how'd you feel about us being neighbors?"

"Get out of here," Annie said, tossing the gift box to the side. "Here? On the island?"

Vicky nodded. "Haven't you heard the construction going on over yonder?" Vicky motioned the direction with her head.

Annie furrowed her brows. "Why, yes, of course we have. We discussed it, but we just weren't sure what it was about. During our September barbecue we saw framing going up over there. Is that you?" Annie widened her eyes.

Vicky tipped her head. "Yes, we're so excited. It just happened. We wanted to live out here, but had no idea it would be next door."

"Well, it will be nice to have some neighbors. It gets dark and lonely out here sometimes."

"Scott is looking forward to having Jack as a neighbor, too."

Annie giggled. She could hear Jack's voice in her head. Major Scott Collins, he'd say. "Well, I don't know how much help I can be, but Jack is very handy with a hammer. Please let us know if there's anything we can do." Annie smiled and then turned to the friend who handed her the next gift to open.

JACK REMAINED COMMITTED to building things for the baby's room, and soon the cradle had a matching dresser and changing table, as well as a crib for when he or she outgrew the cradle. Annie had to remind him to take it slow and learn to enjoy quiet times. He worked too hard and never rested. He teased her that life was for living, and he would make every moment count.

It was during one of their quiet moments that he broke the news to her. "I'm quitting the family business."

Annie, shocked with his revelation, tried to make sense of it before she replied. "What do you mean you're quitting the family business? You're not going to drive anymore?"

Jack shook his head. "I discussed it with Mom and Dad and they're cool with it. I'm going to open my own woodworking shop."

Annie leaned forward and studied his face. "Don't get me wrong, you do beautiful work. Anyone would be lucky to have one of your pieces, but do you think we have room for two entrepreneurs in the family?"

"Yes, I do, and I'm glad you said that. I've been doing some research, and just like your cupcake business, woodworking is very popular here. People love hand-made one-of-a-kind items." He beamed with happiness.

"Okay, because we're having a baby, and we'll need money. I'm going to cut back my hours as I get further along," she said, feeling him out about this new endeavor.

"Not to worry, Dad said if we need extra money, I can do some driving gigs in between. But I feel really good about this venture."

Annie nodded. "Okay, then, if you feel good about it then so do I."

The winters weren't long or severe in South Carolina,

so soon spring was knocking on their door, which meant flowering shrubs and trees and boat rides along the coastal waterway. Annie didn't have to wait too long either.

"Now, give me your hand," Jack said, helping Annie get into the boat.

Annie stepped down, wobbling back and forth before she found her balance.

"Steady, girl," Jack said, laughing.

Annie sat down and waited for Jack to start the engine. Soon they were off. Annie leaned her head back and drew in the fresh air through her nostrils. The wind blew her hair around and she didn't care for a second. She placed one hand on her belly. "Your first boat ride."

Jack pulled back on the throttle and the two just casually trolled along.

"Look at the azaleas, aren't they beautiful?" Annie pointed to the many that could be seen growing on people's properties.

Jack pointed to the white lacy blossoms on the tops of some trees. "Dogwoods," he said.

"We have a couple on our property, too," she said, tipping her head.

After a glorious afternoon on the water, the two headed back.

"I'm going to lie down for a while," she announced as

she made her final step up to the front porch, breathing heavily.

"Yes, you do that. I'll get dinner ready. How do grilled burgers sound?"

"Anything you make sounds great," she tilted her chin and waited for his kiss.

As June approached, Annie and Jack awaited the birth of their first child. Her tummy grew quite a bit during the last couple of weeks. So much so that she couldn't see her toes, and resorted to slip-on shoes so she wouldn't have to bend over to fasten them. All her clothes were big and loose, accommodating her growing size and the temperature as it heated up. She turned this way and that way, looking in the mirror. Her body had transformed so much over the past several weeks.

It was like most typical days. She woke up a bit tired, ate a small breakfast, and just piddled around the house. Jack had been working out in the garage and came in to take a lunch break. It was warm out, and since neither of them really was that hungry, they decided on just some cheese and crackers.

"Let's go eat under the shade tree, shall we?" He held out his arm for her.

They'd just sat down at the picnic table and a cool breeze came up from the shore and brushed past them, making Annie squeal with excitement. She brushed her hair back off her shoulders, and reaching into the pocket of her maternity top, pulled out a rubber band. She tossed her hair in a ponytail and went to reach for a cracker, when she felt the warm liquid trickle down her leg. "Jack."

Jack studied her face. "Yes?"

"It's time."

Jack picked up his leg and tossed it over the bench, standing. "Time? Time as in now … time for the baby?" His breathing became labored and he stuttered.

"Yes, calm down. Help me off the bench," she said calmly.

They held hands as they crossed toward the front porch. "Grab my overnight bag. It's by the door. I'll wait right here."

Jack took two steps at a time to reach the front door. He was back in a flash with her bag. At first, he tore out of the driveway like a madman. But after she talked to him calmly, he settled down. They arrived at the hospital and were ushered in to the examining room. Jack paced the room while the doctors examined her.

"The baby is crowning," the doctor announced.

"The baby is coming, Annie, did you hear that?"

After about twenty minutes of pushing, out came the bright red bundle of joy, screaming at the top of its lungs.

"Congratulations, Mr. and Mrs. Powell, you are the proud parents of a bouncing baby boy!"

Jack leaned up against Annie as she held their baby. His smile beamed clear across the room. He reached down and touched his little fingers. "He's beautiful."

Annie nodded. "Yes, he is, our beautiful little boy. Now you won't feel so outnumbered with me, Buffy, and Isla." She giggled.

"What are you naming him?" the nurse that stood nearby asked.

Annie gazed up to Jack and nodded.

Jack sighed as he studied the little bundle, sending shivers up Annie's spine. She loved him so much and now they had a son together. Her heart felt as if it were going to burst from all the happiness.

"I had two names picked out, but after I saw him, I knew what it should be," he said, looking up at the nurse. "Ashton Robert Powell," he said quietly.

"That's a great name," the nurse said, taking the baby. "I'll be right back with little Ashton."

Jack leaned over and kissed Annie on the mouth. "I love you, honey. How are you feeling?"

"Like I just gave birth to a seven-pound baby boy," she said, giggling.

"I have to go call everyone," Jack said.

Annie placed her hand on his arm. "Go call them. Let everyone know we're doing well and look forward to their visits."

Jack nodded and then he took off out of the room, leaving Annie alone with her thoughts. She was one lucky woman. She knew that and she didn't take a second for granted.

SWEET CAROLINA IS the next book in this series!

ABOUT THE AUTHOR

A USA Today bestselling author, Debbie writes sweet contemporary romance and women's fiction. She lives in South Carolina with her husband and two dachshund rescues, Dash and Briar. An avid supporter of animal rescue, Debbie happily donates a percentage of all book sales to local and national rescue organizations. When you purchase any of her books, you're also helping animals.

To find out more about Debbie, check out her website at https://www.authordebbiewhite.com

BOOKS BY DEBBIE WHITE

Romance Across State Lines

Texas Twosome

Kansas Kissed

California Crush

Oregon Obsession

Romantic Destinations

Finding Mrs. Right

Holding on to Mrs. Right

Cherishing Mrs. Right

Charleston Harbor Novels

Sweet Indulgence

Sweet Magnolia

Sweet Carolina

Sweet Remembrance

Others

Perfect Pitch

Ties That Bind

Passport To Happiness

The Missing ingredient

The Salty Dog

The Pet palace

Billionaire Auction

Billionaire's Dilemma

Coaching the Sub

Christmas Romance – Short Stories

Made in United States
North Haven, CT
02 March 2022

16703888R00134